x   Anderson, Mary   c.1

F*T*C superstar

DATE			
FEB 17 '7?	MAY 1 8 '10		
APR 1 4 '78			
MAY 5 '78			
FEB 2 '79			
DEC 1 4 '79			
FEB 6 '81			
JAN 2 5 '82			
JAN 2 1 '83			
DEC 4 '84			

Mary Anderson

F★T★C★
SUPERSTAR

Illustrated by Gail Owens

Atheneum 1976 New York

To Carl, with ten verys

"I've Got a Gal in Kalamazoo" by Mark Gordon and
Harry Warren. Copyright © 1942 by Twentieth Century
Music Corporation. Copyright renewed 1969. All rights
controlled by Bregman, Vocco & Conn, Inc. Used by
permission. All rights reserved.

Library of Congress Cataloging in Publication Data

Anderson, Mary,   F*T*C* superstar!
SUMMARY: Freddie the Cat discovers a latent acting
talent in himself, but it takes Emma Pigeon to develop
it and make Freddie a star—of commercials.
[1. Acting—Fiction. 2. Advertising—Fiction]
I. Owens, Gail. II. Title. PZ7.A5444Fad
[Fic] 75-30565 ISBN 0-689-30497-8

X
C.I

CONTENTS

Homecoming

Wuzza-wuzza. Wuzza-wuzza. Freddie the Cat lay under the kitchen table as the fan blades spun. He was stretched on the cool tiles, feeling disgusted and depressed. Freddie'd felt miserable ever since returning from vacation three days before.

Hearing the slippered feet of the old folks entering the kitchen, Freddie nuzzled his nose toward the metal dish with his initials, F.M.B. He couldn't touch a bite. As the old lady walked by, she glanced under the table. Freddie's meal of boiled chicken breast was still untouched. She frowned.

"Still not hungry?" she asked with concern. "I can't think what's gotten into you. Take a bite, at least," she coaxed. She pushed his plate closer.

Freddie looked up wistfully. A weak meow escaped his lips. Then he flattened himself out in a listless manner.

"Is that so?" scolded the old lady. "Shame on you, Frederick Morosco Bitterman! That lovely piece of chicken. Plenty of cats in the street would love it."

"Oh, wow," thought Freddie. "The old lady's getting her wind up. She never uses my full name unless she's mad."

An impressive name it was, too. Especially for a cat. Freddie shared the Bitterman with the old folks, but the Frederick Morosco part was his alone.

"You don't fool me," she continued sternly. "Sniffed salmon in my grocery bag, eh? Well, that's for your birthday tomorrow. Not a bite until then."

"*Meeow*," squeaked Freddie. The desire for salmon was far from his mind.

Grabbing the dish from under the table, the old lady placed it in the refrigerator. Relenting, she reopened it and took a brown paper bag from the shelf.

She cut off a generous hunk of salmon, placed it on top of the chicken, then shoved it under the table. "All right," she said sweetly, "but just a little."

"*Meeoww*," Freddie repeated listlessly. He poked the dish with his paw. Then he rolled over and closed his eyes.

"That does it, Herbert," she said nervously. "I'm worried. Freddie's *never* refused salmon."

"Don't fuss over him, Irma," said the old man, sitting by the kitchen table. "It's the heat. I don't feel like eating either."

"Oh no," she said. "It's more than that. Freddie hasn't been himself since we returned from vacation. I think he's homesick."

"How could he be? He *is* home."

"I think he misses the seaside," said Mrs. Bitterman, taking a pitcher of lemonade from the refrigerator. "Maybe he feels cooped up in the apartment."

Freddie's ears perked up as he listened to the old lady. He *was* homesick, but not for the seaside. His yearning went deeper than that. Freddie closed his eyes. For the hundredth time, he pictured the delightful scene that haunted his daydreams . . .

Dusk was falling on the seaside artist colony, as throngs began filling the theater tent. Soon, the bustle of people would subside. Soon the blanket of night would fall. The chain of lights strung beneath the canvas tent would dim. Slowly, the pink and golden spotlights lining the wooden stage would switch on. Then the magic would begin as the actors performed. Soon, the glorious sounds of laughter, excitement and applause would tremble through the canvas walls. Bravo! Bravo! . . .

And to think, mere accident had led Freddie to discover this magical world. When the old folks had chosen the New Jersey town for vacation, it was because old friends had rented a bungalow there, too. As usual, Freddie had planned to spend his two months out of the city relaxing, eating broiled fish and communing with nature. Yet it hadn't taken him long to weary of the porch chitchat and venture off.

Freddie lay under the kitchen table and sighed. How vividly he still remembered the evening he'd discovered The Phoenix Players Troupe. He'd been strolling through the grass, chasing giant ants. Their trail led underneath a wooden structure. Freddie had crawled beneath, following them to their nest hole. As he had placed his paw over the hole, his tail had suddenly quivered with fear. A loud voice shouted overhead. "Touch one hair of Columbine and die!"

Freddie froze. Then he turned and began to crawl from under the planks. But before he got out, a second voice came from above, this one soft and sweet.

"I beg you, sire, be merciful."

The two voices were joined by others. Freddie felt and heard their footsteps pacing above his head. As he slithered from beneath the planking, he noticed rows of feet in front of him. Only then did he realize that he was in a theater. Freddie was an experienced cat who'd lived in Manhattan all his life. But he'd never seen a play. His entertainment had always come from the TV in the old folks' bedroom. He watched soap operas and game shows with the old lady and late-night talk shows with the old man. Seeing *live* actors was something new.

Once he had seen them, he loved them. After that, he had gone to the theater every night. He saw funny plays, sad plays, silly and mad plays. Some he understood, some he didn't. Yet he enjoyed them all. He loved the lights, the sounds, the makeup and costumes. But mostly, he loved the words. He loved one line from one play best of all. "Good king, great king, —and yet, not greatly good." Wow, that was dialogue he'd never heard on soap operas!

Freddie had enjoyed his nightly visits to the theater so much that he had dreaded the thought of returning to the city. Yet, three days ago, that's what had happened. The summer over, he was shoved into the "hot box," dumped on the train and dragged back to Riverside Drive. He'd never see "live" actors again.

"Maybe that salmon's rotten," said Mr. Bitterman, leaning under the table. Freddie gave him a sad glance.

"Fresh from the store this morning," snapped his wife. "Only the best. Our Freddie's sick, Herbert. He always enjoys coming home. Soon as we're in the door, he jumps on the fire escape to find his friends. But he hasn't moved from under the table in three days. It's as if he doesn't care anymore."

The old lady was right again. Freddie didn't care about the same things any more. He wasn't interested in visiting all his 99th Street pals. Usually, Freddie was eager to share his vacation experiences with the sparrow and pigeon families living in the alcove of the building. And being a nosey cat, he had always before been anxious to catch up on the old folks' mail. It gathered in great piles during the summer. Emma Pigeon, the most cultured bird in the neighborhood, lived on the ledge above. She read fluently and always obliged Freddie.

And how Freddie loved to see the children again. He'd notice who had grown tanner, who taller. They enjoyed seeing him, too. "Hi there, Freddie," they'd shout up to his fire escape. "Welcome home."

"Let's take Freddie down to see Miss Lucy," Mrs. Bitterman suggested. "It'll do him good to see an old friend."

Freddie hissed from underneath the table. Miss Lucy was the most spoiled, pampered, pain-in-the-paw Persian in the whole building. The whole world! He was feeling rotten enough without seeing *her*.

"Maybe we should take him to the vet," offered Mr. Bitterman.

Freddie gasped. A visit to the vet meant a shot in the rear, a drop in the eye or a pill on the tongue. That was even worse! He'd better stop schlumping around and act normal. Freddie stretched himself and crawled out from beneath the table. Quickly, he hopped out the kitchen window, onto the fire escape.

"See, Irma," said Mr. Bitterman with relief. "There he goes now. Such a fuss for nothing."

Emma Pigeon

Freddie slouched onto the fire escape. Miss Lucy, indeed. That prescription could *kill* a guy! Oh well, what did *humans* know.

"Hello, Freddie," cooed Emma Pigeon, leaning over the ninth floor ledge. "I didn't know you were back."

"Hi there, Em," said Freddie listlessly. "How are ya?"

"Just splendid," she replied, flying down. "When did you return?"

"Three days ago."

"Three days! I had no idea. I thought surely you'd want your mail read. Why didn't you *psssst* for me? I'm always happy to oblige. You know how I love to read. *Anything.*"

"Yeah," said Freddie, "but I didn't think of it."

"That's strange," said Emma. "You're always so anxious to catch up when you return."

"Guess so," he sighed. "Cats can change, though. Have a good summer, Em?"

"Just lovely," she cooed. "Culturally enriching. I renewed several friendships with the migratory birds in Central Park. I've also continued my studies at the library. I learned about many new subjects. Spelunking. That's examining caves, you know. And philately. Since you love mail, that would interest you. Philately is the study and collection of stamps. Oh, there are dozens of fascinating things I could tell you."

"Some other time," Freddie sighed. "Family well?"

"Excellent," said Emma. "Last month, Willie flew all the way to Chinatown with his father. Dear Clarence is the same as always; constantly seeking new restaurants. He's found a new bakery whose trash cans are the best in town. Oh, Maude spent the summer on a Park Avenue penthouse. It's part of my new

Pigeon Exchange Program. We should travel and observe other birds. It broadens one, don't you agree?"

"Yeah, sure," sighed Freddie, barely listening.

"Summer's lovely," Emma continued. "But Autumn's so invigorating. The children return to school. The libraries buy new books. I could read the Bitterman's mail for you now, Freddie. I haven't read a thing all day."

"No thanks," said Freddie. "Not now."

"What's wrong?" asked Emma, suddenly noticing her friend's sorry state. Freddie wasn't his usual, nosey self. He'd never refused a peek into the old folks' mail before. It was two days till Emma's next trip to the library. She itched to sink her beak into some new reading material. "Aren't you well?" she asked.

"Don't know," said Freddie, drooping his head to his paws. "Been feeling rotten since I got back."

"Didn't you enjoy your vacation? I thought you loved communing with nature."

"I did love it," he said dreamily. "It was the best vacation of my life."

"Then why so unhappy?"

"It's personal," said Freddie. "You wouldn't understand. No one could."

"But I do," Emma insisted. "That's how I felt last

year, remember? Useless and bored. Is that it?"

"Sort of," he confessed.

"Then I do know," said Emma. "And I'd like to help. If you shared your troubles with me . . ."

"No thanks," Freddie interrupted. "No one can help me now. It's too late."

"It's never too late," said Emma. "*You're* the one who taught me that. Remember last spring? It was *your* idea I get interested in reading. That's how I discovered my noble pigeon heritage. Yes, Freddie, I owe everything to you. My whole new life. In some religion I read about, they believe once you save a life, it belongs to you. So, my life is yours, Freddie."

"Hold it, Em. I've got enough trouble handling my own life. Don't dump *yours* on me."

"Our destinies are joined," cooed Emma. "When you feel bad, so do I."

"Ain't no use in *both* of us feeling lousy."

"If only you'd share your troubles," she continued, "perhaps they'd go away."

"It's no use," said Freddie stoically. "It's over. Life has passed me by. Know what day it is tomorrow? My birthday. Know how old I'm gonna be? Six. That's right, Em. Six big ones. Half my life, down the tubes. What've I got to show for it? A metal bowl with F.M.B. and a heavy heart."

"Six isn't old," said Emma. "One year of a cat's

life equals seven human years. That makes you forty-two. That's the prime of life. The peak of maturity. The beginning of productivity, sensitivity, creativity . . ."

"It's the end," he snapped. "There's nothing left for me. Just a wicker bed and a pan of kitty litter beside the stove. Wow, if I had it to do over, it'd be different." Freddie rolled over on his back. He stared at the blue sky as a thick line of white clouds floated by. "I'd see my name up there." He sighed, pointing dreamily. "I'd make people laugh and cry. Everyone would know Freddie, that famous cat." He closed his eyes and whispered softly. "Good king, great king,—and yet, not greatly good."

Emma cocked her head. "That's from Shakespeare," she said. "You want to be a writer? That's not a problem. My Willie knows the alphabet. Perhaps he could teach . . ."

"Good king, great king,—and yet, not greatly good," Freddie repeated, thrusting his paws dramatically.

"I'm sure that's from Shakespeare," Emma muttered. "*Richard II.* I know!" she chirped with excitement. "You want to be an *actor!*"

"You guessed it," said Freddie sadly. "Go ahead and laugh. I don't blame you."

"Oh, I'd never," she said earnestly. "You never laughed at my dreams of being a Carrier Pigeon. We all must have our dreams. Please tell me about yours."

Freddie stared into Emma's eyes. Suddenly, all his emotions came spilling out. He confided each glowing detail of his summer experience. He described his awe of the actors, his joy in the theater world and his hopeless ambition to become part of it. When finished, he breathed a sigh, then curled up beside the coolness of the geranium pots. Sharing his feelings had made him feel better. "That's it," he said. "I'm an alley cat who wants to be an actor. Pathetic, huh?"

"Not at all," Emma replied. "As I said, we all must have our dreams. But why has the theater become yours? You never mentioned being interested in acting."

"Well," said Freddie, licking the dew drops from the geranium leaves, "I was born outside a theater."

"You never told me," said Emma with interest. "In Manhattan?"

"Think so," he said. "All I remember is a large white building with an alley out back. My dad cut out before I was born. Cats do that, sometimes. My mom had to take care of me and my two brothers. One day, she went out searching for food. A few minutes later, I heard the screech of car wheels. There was my mom, lying in the street. Some nut had run her over."

"That's dreadful," said Emma. "We city animals lead such hazardous lives."

"That's when I met the old folks," Freddie continued. "They were on their way into the theater. They saw the accident and noticed me on the sidewalk, meowing like crazy. They took me home where I've been ever since. I guess when I discovered those actors, it brought back my kitten days in the theater alley."

"Quite right," said Emma. "Experiences of youth are the strongest. I read that in *Psychology Today*. You had a latent interest in theater. Probably a latent talent, as well."

"Maybe so," said Freddie. "But who cares? Theater's for people; not for cats."

"Don't be so sure," said Emma. She'd suddenly remembered an article she'd placed in her files. "I may be able to help you, my friend."

"Aw, I'm too old for dreams, anyway," said Freddie, sighing. "That's kid stuff. Me and the old folks'll spend the rest of our years together. We'll pad around the house drinking warm milk and watching soap operas."

"Don't be certain," said Emma fluttering off the fire escape. "It's getting late and I've work to do. I'll be back tomorrow. Keep your chin up until then. Fate and Destiny await!"

Freddie nodded and watched Emma fly away. A swell bird. But she sure talked dopey sometimes.

Miss Lucy

As Freddie stuck his head back in the window, he wished he hadn't. He was going to visit Miss Lucy after all. Mrs. Bitterman insisted. "Seeing an old friend is just the medicine he needs."

The old lady snapped on his leash and escorted him into the elevator. Freddie dragged his paws and drooped his tail. Mrs. Bitterman rang the bell of apartment 3C. Miss Ivers, a short, round, smiley-faced woman answered. Freddie strolled in and sniffed around, noticing the scent of corn muffins. Miss Ivers' apartment *always* smelled of corn muffins.

"Welcome back, Irma," she said. "I've just made a lovely batch of corn muffins. Let's go in the living room and have some with tea. You can tell me about your vacation."

"I brought Freddie, too," said Mrs. Bitterman. "I think he's lonesome for Miss Lucy."

Freddie hissed.

"Isn't that dear," smiled Miss Ivers. "She's in her room. She didn't sleep too well last night. But I'm sure she'd love a visitor."

Miss Ivers picked Freddie up and carried him to the door of Miss Lucy's room. Gently, she opened it. "Miss Lucy," she whispered softly. "A friend has come to visit."

Miss Lucy, a very large, very fat, gray Persian, lay on a satin coverlet on top of a double bed. She opened her slanty blue eyes, and gave Freddie an indifferent glance. Then curling up in a ball, she turned away.

"I'll just close the door," said Miss Ivers softly, dropping Freddie to the floor. "We ladies can have a little chat while the children play together."

Mrs. Bitterman smiled and nodded. The two ladies walked down the hall, leaving Freddie alone in the room with the Persian.

"Hi there, Scarface," snarled Miss Lucy. "You back already? Thought we might be rid of you this time. Where did you tramp off to this year?"

"New Jersey," Freddie replied icily.

"Never been," yawned the cat. "Seen it from my window. Doesn't look like much."

"You don't know what you're missing," said Freddie, trying to act superior. *That* wasn't easy with Miss Lucy! "It's really special," he said, jumping onto her bed.

"Don't come up here!" Miss Lucy hissed. "I'm allergic to cat hairs."

"That's ridiculous," said Freddie. "You *are* a cat."

"But I'm *pedigreed*," Miss Lucy purred. "It's *alley cat* hairs that bother me."

"What d'ya want me to do? Shave?"

"An improvement," she hissed, "but hardly necessary. Just sit over there by the air purifier." Through her slanty eyes, Miss Lucy watched Freddie stretch out on the edge of the rug. "So tell me," she continued, "did you go crawling around those gritty beaches as usual?"

"Sometimes."

"Hmm," she said, stretching herself. "So I see. Your paws are still packed with sand."

Freddie glanced down. Several sandy patches still

remained between his pads. "It takes a while to get rid of it," he said. He quickly began licking his paddy-paws.

"Must you do that?" asked Miss Lucy. "It's disgusting."

"Don't know another way," said Freddie, continuing his wash.

"Personally, I prefer a weekly bath." She sighed. "In bubbly oils, of course. Mustn't dry out my sensitive skin. But I suppose alley cats know nothing of cleanliness."

"I'm not an alley cat," Freddie snapped. "I'm a house cat, same as you. In better shape, too. Don't get any fatter, old girl. They'll have to roll you to your bowl."

"Persians are supposed to be plump. It's becoming."

"Well you're becoming bigger every day. No wonder you never leave this room. Betcha can't get your big body off the bed."

"I wouldn't dream of leaving this bed," she said haughtily. "Not while you're in my room."

"Wasn't my idea to come," said Freddie. "My old lady's."

"Must you refer to Mrs. Bitterman in that manner? It's so undignified. The ladies are our *people*. They deserve our respect. They care for us. They *feed* us. It's difficult finding good people; especially for someone like myself. I've such delicate tastebuds. Foods must be prepared just so. Nothing but the best. And with all my allergies, things must be kept spotless. Miss Ivers does quite nicely. In return, I fill her drab, dull life with joy and happiness."

"So that's what ya do," said Freddie. "I never noticed."

"We cats must look out for ourselves in this world," she continued. "Don't you agree?"

"I used to," said Freddie. "But now I'm not sure. Maybe doing things for others is even better."

"Doing for others?" Miss Lucy laughed. "Such as what?"

"Making them laugh, maybe," said Freddie. "Or even cry."

"Who wants to cry?" she sneered. "With my allergies, my eyes tear up enough. Besides, cats aren't meant to do things. Things should be done for them."

"Why do I talk to you," Freddie snapped. He jumped on the bed beside the Persian, pointing an accusing paw. "Look at you!" he shouted. "All soaped up and brushed down. No thoughts in your fat head. What do you know about dreams?" he screeched. "Or Shakespeare. Or *life!*" Freddie slumped down and began mumbling. "Good king, great king,—and yet, not greatly good."

Miss Lucy gave a startled glance. "Definitely disturbed," she hissed, then proceeded to slide off the bed. She placed her left paw out, but suddenly froze in her tracks. She'd just noticed two dust particles stuck between her claws. "AAGGHH!!" she screeched hysterically. "Soot! You've gotten soot all over me!"

"So you've got a sooty foot. So what?"

"Get out of my room this instant," she hissed, crawling up on the opposite side of the bed. She arched her back and bared her teeth.

Suddenly, the bedroom door swung open, and the two old women entered. "What's happening?" asked Miss Ivers. "Miss Lucy dear, you seem upset."

Freddie hissed his nastiest hiss. Then he swatted the fat cat with his claw. Miss Lucy crawled meekly to the edge of the bed, meowing in a pitifully weak voice.

The two women stared at the cats. "Whatever it was," said Mrs. Bitterman apologetically, "it seems it was Freddie's fault. He hasn't been behaving since we returned."

"What a shame," said Miss Ivers. She sat down beside Miss Lucy, gently stroking her fur. "Perhaps a visit to the vet," she suggested. Miss Lucy dropped her head onto her owner's lap and continued to meow softly. "They're such sensitive souls. The slightest thing upsets them. Especially purebreds. They demand the best."

"Thanks for the corn muffins, Edith," said Mrs. Bitterman. She snapped Freddie's leash onto his collar. "I'll call you in the morning."

Miss Ivers raised the Persian's paw in a gesture of farewell. "Say bye-bye," she coaxed. Miss Lucy screwed up her face into an evil-looking smile and purred softly. Then Freddie was escorted from the room and into the elevator.

"How was the visit?" asked Mr. Bitterman when his wife returned.

"Not so great," she said, placing Freddie on the sofa. She rolled him over on his back and began scratching his belly. It was the one thing Freddie couldn't resist; three strokes up, three down, three to the side. He purred with pleasure, forgetting horrible Fat Lucy.

"Ah," said Mrs. Bitterman, nodding. "That makes you feel better, doesn't it? That's what my Fredsy-Wedsy needs; a good scratch on the tum-tum." Freddie closed his eyes in enjoyment. "And tomorrow," the old lady added, "you'll get your special party hat to wear on Fredsy-Wedsy's birthday. And a big bowl of salmon soaked in butter. Only the best."

Freddie suddenly opened his eyes in shocked awareness. His old lady talked just like Miss Ivers! He'd never noticed that before. That made him just like Miss Lucy—a spoiled, pampered, selfish pet. Is that all he had to look forward to in life? Growing fat and getting allergies!

Freddie let out a long moan, jumped off the sofa and dashed underneath the kitchen table. He remained there, refusing to come out, no matter how hard the old lady coaxed.

"I tell you, Herbert," said Mrs. Bitterman. "There's something weird going on with that cat!"

The Ledge

When Emma flew back to her ledge, she found her husband Clarence and his pal, Roscoe the Sparrow, waiting there. Wednesday was their day on the town, so she hadn't expected them till later. Clarence was propped up against the wall's edge, his feet spread in the air, his stomach bulging. There was a glazed look in his eyes and a self-satisfied grin by his beak.

"Some day, wasn't it, Clarence," said Roscoe, stretched beside him. "Did you ever see so many hot dog buns?"

"Never," said Clarence. "And how's about those french fries. And potato chips. And popcorn. Those Italian ices were the greatest."

Emma shook her head and frowned. "I see you two've been at it again," she said. "Gorging. Where'd you go this time?"

"Coney Island," said Roscoe. "It's a paradise. There's so much food on the ground, it'd take an army to eat it all."

"You flew all the way to Brooklyn?" asked Emma.

"*One* way," said Clarence, laughing. "Right, Roscoe?"

"Yeah." He smiled. "After eating all day, we were too full to make the flight back. We hitched a ride."

"Clarence, you didn't," said Emma.

"It wasn't bad," he explained. "Gets a little scarey going under tunnels, but it sure beats walking. After four Nathan's hot dogs, I couldn't get myself off the ground."

"But that's so dangerous," she said.

"Not really," Roscoe argued. "We were careful. But it's a good thing we didn't take Crazy Larry along."

"Sure is," agreed Clarence. "What a show-off bird.

Always playing "chicken" in front of cars. I heard he's grounded for a month. Got a broken wing. Even Nathan's ain't worth losing your health."

"Clarence," scolded Emma, "you're to promise never to do that again."

"Now, Em," he said, "we've got an agreement. Wednesday's my day to do what I like. You started this open marriage stuff after you read about it. I never yell when you stay up late reading your files. Sometimes, I think your eyes are gonna pop out. But that's your business. Stuffing myself is mine."

"But cars have always made me nervous," she explained. "Freddie's mother was *killed* by one. He told me so himself, just minutes ago."

"So Freddie's back, eh?" said Roscoe. "Bet he dragged you down to read all the Bitterman's mail. He's sure a nosey cat."

"Not this time," said Emma. "Freddie's feeling rather poorly. He's got a problem, and I've promised to help him with it."

"Now, Em, you're not gonna start on one of your *projects*, are you? I haven't recovered from that Carrier Pigeon idea."

"I merely plan to help the poor animal fulfill his fate."

"Sounds heavy to me," whispered Roscoe. "I think you're in for a big deal, Clarence."

"Yeah," he agreed. "Sure glad I'm starting on a full stomach."

"Full is hardly the word," snapped Emma. "*Bulging* would be more appropriate. It's a positive *protuberance.*"

Clarence leaned over to Roscoe. "Emma's up to the *p*'s in her dictionary," he explained.

"I suggest you two get some sleep," said Emma. "Then in the morning, perhaps a few flights around the wading pool might eliminate that paunch."

"I haven't seen the kids yet," he said. "Where'd they go?"

"Sleeping at Monica Pigeon's roost," Emma explained. "They're in the 101st Street Racing Competition tomorrow, along with Priscilla and Nan. No need to stay up. I've research on the roof. You needn't wait for me, either."

"Are you going to the Olson penthouse *again*," said Clarence.

"Certainly. Freddie's problem is serious. No time to lose. I must help before total depression sets in. I read that in *Psychology Today.*"

"So what's his trouble?" asked Roscoe.

"He's suffering from an acute case of ego-deflation, compounded by a sudden awareness of Thesbian potentials."

"What's that mean?" asked Roscoe.

"It means I was wrong," said Clarence, as he tried to roll over into a more comfortable position. "Emma's passed the *p*'s in her dictionary. She must be on the *t*'s already."

"Thesbian," Emma recited. (Having a photographic memory, she retained everything.) "Of or characteristic of Thespis, sixth-century Greek poet. Pertaining to tragedy or the dramatic art in general. A tragedian: an actor or actress."

"I think she's saying Freddie wants to act," explained Clarence.

"Cats can't act," said Roscoe, laughing.

"And pigeons can't read," said Emma haughtily. "There are exceptions to everything. Some aspire to higher heights. We're not content to merely scrounge, glut and gorge."

"I think Em means you should mind your own business," explained Clarence.

"Yeah, well it's getting late," said Roscoe awkwardly. "I'd better fly to my roost."

"I suggest you walk," said Emma. "You're in no condition to fly."

"Maybe you're right," he said, lifting himself up a little. "It was fun, Clarence. Let's do it again next Wednesday."

"See you around," said Clarence. He tried getting up, but his stomach was much too full. Instead, he waved a wing in Roscoe's direction, then rolled over and closed his eyes.

As Roscoe cautiously walked around a corner of the ledge, Emma heard a sound suspiciously resembling a burp.

Once Clarence was asleep, Emma flew to the penthouse ledge above. This was her home away from home; the private spot she'd created for herself. Fortunately, it was a section none of the birds considered ideal roosting ground. Though the cornice was broad with ample room underneath, the occupant of the penthouse, Mr. Olson, was a writer with peculiar working hours. He slept during the day and worked at night. The noise from his electric typewriter and the lights from his window made it an awful place for birds to sleep. But it was the perfect site for Emma's office. She could sit all night, reading by Mr. Olson's lamplight.

Apart from her children, Willie and Maude, Emma's files were her greatest pride. She'd taught her family to read, but only she truly loved it. Each morning when the trash was placed beside the building, Emma eagerly fluttered down to leaf through magazines. Monday morning held the biggest treat, when people threw out their big fat Sunday *New York Times*.

Not everything Emma read got carried to her files. She had neither the time, space nor strength for that. Instead she ripped the most interesting articles from the paper with her beak, then page by page delivered them to the roof.

Emma had arranged everything alphabetically according to topic. Rocks were placed on top of each category, so nothing could be blown away. Freddie had kindly provided the rocks. He had also contributed the old folks' *National Geographic* magazines, plus a strip of plastic sheeting to keep things dry. The ledge was quite broad, so Emma's files continued to grow.

Over the months, she'd learned the tastes of all her neighbors. Mr. Mankowitz, an amateur inventor, subscribed to *Popular Mechanics*. Mrs. Mankowitz provided *Woman's Day*, *Family Circle* and *McCalls*. Mr. Cohen, the psychologist, contributed *Psychology Today*, and his wife supplied the movie magazines. Mr. Ungar loved *Gourmet* magazine. Even Maude occasionally read the articles in *MS*, supplied by the girls on the third floor.

But it was to her theater file that Emma flew this evening. This had been contributed by Arnee Cleaver, a young actor living in the hotel next door. In this file, Emma had collected articles from *Variety*, the "Theater Arts" section of the *Times*, posters and playbills. There was also a thumb-worn copy of *An Actor Prepares* with a broken binding.

Emma rolled the rock over, then leafed through the articles until she found the one she wanted. She settled down with this by the lamplight, glancing at each page, first with one eye, then the other. Occasionally, she nodded to herself and smiled. "Just as I thought," she mumbled. Finally she selected a pencil from the paper cup of stubs in the corner, placed it in her beak, and put a check by sections of the article. "Won't Freddie be thrilled," she muttered.

Her research complete, Emma put the article in her beak and flew back home. Clarence was still fast asleep. Dreaming of giant Nathan's hot dogs, no doubt. Quietly, she placed the paper beneath her pillow of twigs. She smiled, then drifted off to sleep.

Happy Birthday

The next day was Freddie's birthday. To his disgust,
he was forced to wear his party hat. Mrs. Bitterman
had bought the awful thing the day he came to live
with them, September 7, six years before. She'd been
dragging it out every year since.

When he was a kitten, Freddie thought the hat
adorable. He loved to play with the bells on the end

of its red velvet top. But it was old and chewed-up now. Worst of all, it looked like a *clown's* hat.

Freddie lay beside his birthday bowl of uneaten broiled salmon, the bells of his hat slopping into the butter sauce. Emma Pigeon fluttered onto the ledge outside.

"Are you in there, Freddie?" she called. She dropped her papers to the windowsill, clamping them with her claws.

"No," said Freddie solemnly.

"Please come out," she coaxed. "I've something to tell you."

"Go away," he grumbled, trying to scrunch his face under his hat. "I won't see anybody. And no one's to see me."

"It's dreadfully important," Emma insisted.

"All right," said Freddie. "But if ya laugh, I'll bite your beak off."

Freddie slunk out from beneath the table. He walked slowly toward the window, his tail tucked between his paws. His soiled, tattered hat hung over his eyes. The bells knocked him in the face. The elastic below his chin puffed his cheeks into fat, furry balls.

Emma forced back a smile. "You look charming," she said tactfully. "The perfect costume for an actor."

"I look like a fool," he grunted, leaping to the win-dowsill.

"Shakespeare wrote a great part for a fool," said Emma. "In *King Lear*."

"Oh yeah," said Freddie. "Bet it wasn't a cat."

"Well, no. But playwrights have written parts for animals for centuries. The ancient Greek playwright, Aristophanes, wrote four plays for them: *The Lark, The Wasps, The Birds* and *The Frogs*."

"Don't believe it," said Freddie. "Never seen bugs and frogs on stage."

"But it's true," said Emma. "It says so in this arti-cle. Modern theater's filled with animal parts, too." She began reading her list. "*The Male Animal, The Glass Menagerie, The Animal Kingdom*. Here's one called *The Seven Year Itch*."

"What's that about? Fleas?"

"Perhaps," said Emma. "And there are more: *The Hairy Ape, Beggar on Horseback, The Wild Duck, The Seagull, Hogan's Goat, Androcles and the Lion, The Bat*. Here's three of interest to you, Freddie: *Of Mice and Men, The Mousetrap* and *Rats*."

"But how about cats?" he asked. "Any starring cats?"

"Yes," said Emma. "One called *Cat on a Hot Tin Roof*."

"What d'ya know," he shouted. "I'd never have

believed it."

"And I haven't finished the list," said Emma. There's a play called *The Little Foxes* and another called *Rhinoceros*. And two about pigs: *Porgy* and *Pygmalion*. There's one called *Jumpers*. Perhaps that stars kangaroos?

"Hold it, Em," Freddie interrupted. "So there's a place for animals in acting. But how'd they get there? Did all those apes, goats and pigs just walk on stage? They must've been special guys to get plays written for them."

"Perhaps they went to school first," Emma suggested. "Acting school. That's what Arnee Cleaver does. He works part time and takes acting lessons at night."

"I knew there was a catch," said Freddie sullenly. "You've gotta be a *rich cat*. My old folks don't have no money. I'm back where I started," he said gloomily. "Getting old and going nowhere."

"I've got it!" Emma chirped. "*I* can teach you, Freddie."

"You're no actor, Em."

"But Arnee Cleaver is," she explained. "I've got all his notes and books. I could read them and teach you what I learn. Perhaps I flatter myself, but I've always thought I was a clever pigeon."

"Oh, you *are*," said Freddie. "The best. But

wouldn't it take lots of work?"

"Good things are worth the effort. Besides, I'd enjoy the challenge. Frankly, Freddie, I'm getting weary of the library. It's rather lonesome. Think of it. I'd be a teacher with my very own pupil. Isn't it exciting!"

"Ya mean you'd enjoy teaching me stuff?"

"I'd love it," she said.

"Oh boy!" Freddie shouted. "My birthday's not a bust after all."

"We can start tomorrow," chirped Emma. "Twelve o'clock sharp. Go in and enjoy your party now, Freddie. I'll see you then."

Freddie waved his paw excitedly as Emma flew back to her roost. The heavy lump he'd had in his stomach suddenly disappeared. He felt hungry again. Remembering the delicious plate of broiled salmon awaiting him, he eagerly jumped through the window.

Mrs. Bitterman was passing the kitchen as Freddie dashed underneath the table and began devouring his birthday meal. "Herbert!" she shouted with delight. "Freddie's better. He's finally eating."

"That's nice, Irma," replied her husband from the living room. "That's real nice."

Family Agreement

At dinner that evening, the Pigeon family sat around their paper napkin table, eating their meal of bread crusts. Emma waited for a suitable moment to discuss her new project.

"What's for dessert, Em?" asked Clarence, gobbling down his portion.

Emma hopped to the cardboard box that served as their cupboard. She checked the slivers remaining in the cast-off cellophane bags. "Potato chips or Cheez Doodles."

"No sugar-roasted nuts?" he asked disappointedly.

"I was saving them for Sunday dinner," she said, "but I'll serve them if you like."

"Yummy," said Willie. "I sure worked up an appetite today."

"How was the race?" asked Emma, dropping two nuts beside each place.

"Maude cheated," said Willie. "That's why she came in first."

"Did not cheat," Maude shouted. "You always say that when I win. I'm faster and stronger than you."

"Girls can't be stronger," Willie shouted. "That's why they cheat."

"I'm sure you both did admirably," said Emma. "Was there a prize?"

"Sure was," said Maude. "A plastic checker and two baseball cards. I gave them all to Whiney-Willie."

"Well, I'm the one who collects them," he argued. "Anyway, you only got them cause you cheated."

"Did not."

"Did so."

"Would you care for my dessert, Clarence?" Emma cooed.

"Sure. You know I'm nuts about peanuts."

"What a clever joke, dear," she said, rolling the

nuts in his direction. "You certainly have a sharp sense of humor."

"Never mentioned it before," he said suspiciously. "What's on your mind?"

"Nothing," said Emma lightly. "I've just begun to notice things lately. Take Willie and Maude, for instance. They're growing so quickly. They hardly need me in the roost at all."

"You're driving at something, Em. What is it?"

"I merely meant, that if I were gone all afternoon, no one would miss me."

"We have an agreement," said Clarence. "Trips to the library only twice a week."

"But this is something different," she said. "A fascinating new project."

"And it's name is Freddie the Cat. Now I know why I got your nuts. A bribe. What're you gonna do? Move in on the poor guy and make him over?"

"Exactly," said Emma. "I'm his new acting coach."

"A cat can't be an actor, Ma," said Willie.

"Yes he can," she argued. "He can be whatever he likes, if he works hard enough."

"There's no place for animals in show business," said Clarence.

"That's where you're wrong," said Emma. She told her family all the facts she'd learned. Then she listed all the plays written for animals. Willie and Maude were fascinated. Clarence was skeptical.

"You're crazy, Em. Nothing personal, but that's the screwiest idea ever. You must've read wrong."

"It makes perfect sense," said Emma. "Freddie and I plan to work each afternoon until he knows everything my acting books can teach him."

"That's swell," said Maude. "Women are fighting for equal rights. Why shouldn't cats?"

"You've been reading that mizzy magazine again," Willie said.

"Well, it's true," Maude argued. "Go ahead and do it, Mom. It'll be great having a celebrity in the building. Maybe I'll ask for his autograph."

"You'll have to teach him to write first," Willie said.

"That could be *your* job, William," Emma suggested. "When Freddie becomes known, he'll need to give out autographs."

"Hey, that's right," said Willie. "I'm awful good at printing."

"I could teach Freddie about makeup and dress-up," Maude offered. "I know lots about lipstick and high heels. I listen to the ladies in the park."

"That would be most helpful, dear," Emma cooed.

"How about you, Pop?" asked Willie. "What're *you* gonna do for Freddie?"

"Keep my mouth shut," said Clarence. He hopped to the cupboard and browsed through with his beak. "Any nuts left? I need them to settle my nerves."

The Lessons Begin

That night, Emma remained on the penthouse for
hours. She read through her theater file, creating a
lesson plan. The next day, notes in her beak, she flew
to Freddie's windowsill. He was lying in the afternoon sun, licking his paws. He'd just had a lovely
lunch of chicken livers. Freddie's appetite had returned, along with his good humor.

"Hi, Em." He smiled. "Can hardly wait to start school. Look out, show biz, here I come!"

"Actors aren't made overnight," Emma cautioned. "There's hard work ahead. For our first lesson, let's refer to Stanislavski."

"Stan-whosky?"

"Stanislavski. The famous Russian actor and director," Emma explained. "He's considered a master teacher. He says the first thing an actor must remember is that there can be no true art without living."

"I've lived like crazy," said Freddie proudly. "Six big ones, Em, remember?"

"A point in your favor. Now, we'll begin with a simple exercise. First, an actor must learn to use his imagination. Lie back, look up at the sky and tell me what you see."

Freddie lay on his back, glancing at the white fleecy clouds above. "A zipper," he said. "Those skinny clouds look just like the zippers on the old man's pants."

"That's all?" asked Emma. "No pre-historic shapes? No fancy figures?"

"Just a zipper, Em. Is that bad?"

"Perhaps we'll try listening instead. Pay attention to the wind in the trees. What does it sound like?"

Freddie pointed his ears. "Bacon," he said. "Sizzling in the pan."

"Freddie, your thoughts must be more artistic."

"Still sounds like bacon to me. Wow, it's great just from the pan; one side lean, the other floppy."

"Let's continue," sighed Emma. "Have you a mirror?"

"The old lady keeps one on her dresser," he said. "I'll get it." Freddie hopped through the window and returned with a hand mirror in his mouth. "The old lady's out shopping," he explained. "She'll never miss it."

"That's fine," said Emma, referring to her notes. "Stanislavski says to be careful with a mirror. It teaches an actor to watch the outside rather than the inside."

"I've never seen inside," said Freddie. "Except when I cut myself. Then what's inside squishes out. I guess that's what Stan meant; don't cut yourself with your mirror."

"Possibly," said Emma, reading further. "Showing your teeth and rolling the whites of your eyes shows jealousy. Practice that, Freddie."

"Okay," he said, staring into the mirror. He popped his eyes. He grit his teeth. He even hissed a little. "This is fun," he said, "but the eye-rolling part makes me dizzy."

"That's enough," said Emma. "Now, let's try some body exercises. Roll over a few times."

"Okay," he said, tucking his paws together. "Here I go." Freddie rolled toward the end of the fire escape, smashing his nose against the geranium pots. "Ouch!" he groaned, soothing the bruise with his paddy-paw.

"This space is too small," said Emma. "Especially for ballet."

"Ballet?" shouted Freddie. "I ain't gonna do no tippy-toe stuff."

"Now, Frederick, you want to learn properly."

"Well, yeah," he pouted.

"Then promise you'll try some ballet this evening. Nothing difficult; just some toe stands. I'm sure you've seen them on TV."

"Okay," he said reluctantly. "But keep it under your beak. Not a word to anyone."

"Agreed," said Emma. "Well now, I'd say that was a fine first lesson."

"I did good, huh?" said Freddie proudly. "Wanna see the eye-rolling part again? How's about the hiss?"

"Save them for this evening," Emma suggested. "That's part of your homework. I'll be back at noon tomorrow to find out how you did."

"Okay," said Freddie. He waved good-bye as Emma fluttered to the ledge above.

Late that evening, as promised, Freddie began his homework. Cautiously, he tiptoed into the bedroom.

The old folks were stretched out in bed, dozing through the late night TV news.

Freddie jumped onto the dresser and stared into the hand mirror. By the light of the television, he could see his face clearly. Slowly, he rolled his eyes. He exposed his teeth. He hissed menacingly. Freddie was so busy making his crazy faces, he never noticed the old man wake up. Mr. Bitterman stared in surprise. Freddie continued making wild-eyed, insane faces into the mirror.

When that part of his lesson was complete, Freddie hopped down from the dresser. Suddenly, he began tumbling across the floor. Mr. Bitterman grabbed for his eyeglasses, just as Freddie's head hit the wall a third time. The cat got up and shook himself off.

The sound of applause could be heard from the television set. "And now, here's Johnny!" shouted the announcer. Mr. Bitterman stared open-mouthed. The silhouette of Freddie the Cat began to tippy-dance in front of his screen. Freddie stood on his hind legs, his front paws above his head. Gracefully, he tippy-toed across the room, completing two perfect pirouettes.

"Irma," shouted Mr. Bitterman as he shook his wife. "Wake up. The cat's having an attack!"

Freddie came to a sudden stop. The old lady roused herself from sleep. "What'd you say?" she asked grogily, adjusting her chin strap.

"It's Freddie. He's having some kind of fit."

Mrs. Bitterman glanced at the cat. Freddie was resting beside the TV, relaxed and innocent.

"Nothing wrong with Freddie," she said sharply. "Must've been a nightmare, Herbert. Don't eat salami before bed." She rolled over and went back to sleep.

Mr. Bitterman stared at Freddie. "I could've sworn I saw that cat . . . ah, he couldn't have." He got up, flicked off the TV and went back to bed.

And the
Lessons Continue

Before long, the entire 99th Street ledge was atwitter with gossip about Emma Pigeon's new "project."

"She's running a regular *school* down there," chirped Roscoe the Sparrow. "She and Freddie have their heads together every day."

"Spells trouble," grumbled Sanford Pigeon, the oldest of the group. "In my day, we steered clear of cats. Can't trust them."

"Emma knows what she's doing," said Monica Pigeon. "But she's looking awfully tired."

"It's overwork," said Monica's husband, Gilbert. "That bird can't pace herself."

"What's it all for?" chirped the sparrows.

"What's the reason?" twittered the baby pigeons.

"Silly nonsense," added Sanford.

"I feel sorry for her husband," tweeted Grace, a visiting starling from New Jersey. "Mine would never allow such goings-on. Spending all that time with a *cat*. It's not normal!"

Yet, as the days passed, Clarence became resigned to the affair. Emma was always back by three o'clock. Meals were prompt as usual. Actually, Emma's absence from the ledge gave him more time to goof off with Roscoe.

Though Clarence disagreed with his wife, he admired her. for sticking with it. He showed this in small, personal gestures. Sometimes, he'd sweep the ledge in the morning, letting Emma grab some extra sleep. Each Tuesday, his night to prepare dinner, he'd put decorative sprigs of dandelion weeds beside his wife's place setting. And often, he'd scrounge up some extra-special dessert. Emma would smile and say, "Thank you." Clarence would grunt and say, "Forget it."

Willie and Maude helped, too. Each afternoon, Willie flew down to give Freddie a writing lesson. Not skilled enough to scratch out Frederick Morosco Bitterman, Willie knew the cat couldn't, either. Instead, they settled for initials. Willie copied the F.M.B. from the cat's bowl. But the *M* was too hard for Freddie. All those up and down strokes never met in the right place. F.T.C., meaning Freddie the Cat was far easier to learn. Soon Freddie had finished the F and was halfway through the T.

Maude's makeup lessons were also helpful. She taught Freddie about eyeliner, face cream and lipstick. Her explanation of how to apply face powder was so fascinating, Freddie decided to try it. Powder was one of the few cosmetics the old lady used, and Freddie knew just where she kept it. That afternoon, while Mrs. Bitterman was in the kitchen, Freddie pulled open her dresser drawer. He lifted the lid from the powder box and found the puff inside. Picking it up, he smacked himself in the nose. Flecks of powder scattered everywhere. Freddie choked from the taste. He ran around the floor, frantically wiping his face into the rug. Later, Mrs. Bitterman found him stretched out on the bed, clumps of powder stuck to his eyebrows and nose. "What're you up to now?" she said, laughing. "I swear, you're becoming a *peculiar* cat."

But for the most part, Freddie's lessons went smoothly. Emma had already completed a brief history of the theater, including the Greek playwrights and Shakespeare. There were lessons on theater slang, theater superstitions and famous theater people. It took Freddie a while to understand the difference between rep and stock, improvisation and motivation; to realize "break a leg" meant good luck and "good luck" meant bad. But Emma sat with him for hours until he'd learned it all.

Freddie especially enjoyed Emma's lesson on vaudeville. She explained about variety acts, including tap dancing with a straw hat and cane. Freddie was anxious to try it, so he shoved the flip tops from soda cans between his claws. Unfortunately, some fell off, while others just hung from his nails. Freddie was also fascinated by the soft shoe and sand dance. A dancer would drop a handful of sand onto the ground, then shuffle around on it, making a gritty, musical sound.

That night, Freddie practiced it himself. First, he borrowed Mr. Bitterman's summer straw hat. Then he dumped all the sand out of Mrs. Bitterman's cactus plants and began to dance around in it. But the sand got stuck between his paddies, as it always did. Sighing, he gave up, flipped his food bowl on his head and began his posture walk. Slowly, he tippy-toed back

and forth across the kitchen tiles. When he grew
tired, he turned the bowl upside down, like a hat. It
was easier that way.

Next morning, the old lady discovered his mess.
Freddie's telltale paw prints were tracked through the
overturned cactus pots. Freddie himself was lying fast
asleep against the kitchen wall. Mr. Bitterman's straw
hat lay by his side. The food bowl was still on his
head. Mrs. Bitterman frowned. Freddie was getting
weirder every day!

During the third week of school, Emma gave Freddie voice instruction: proper diction and singing. As
she explained, "an actor's voice is his most precious
tool. And yours, Freddie, is badly in need of repair.
First, you've got to put your voice into your mask.
That's the front of your face. This exercise always
helps. Place marbles in your mouth while you speak."

"Ain't got marbles," said Freddie, "just a rubber
ball. I'll get it." Freddie returned with the ball and
placed it in his mouth.

"Repeat after me," said Emma. "My name is Freddie."

"Moy nae iss Eeiy," he replied.

"That's not right."

"Atz owt ide," Freddie repeated.

"That ball's no good," said Emma. "Sure you
haven't any marbles?"

"How's about my Pussy Pellet Balls? The old folks leave them for me to snack." He jumped in the window and returned with a mouthful. "Ow's iss, Emm?" he asked. "An ooo eere ee?"

"You're not supposed to *swallow* them," said Emma sharply.

"But they're yummy," said Freddie. "What a swell exercise."

"Let's continue," said Emma, feeling an ache in her feathers. "The next step in speech is knowing when *not* to speak. These moments are called the logical and psychological pauses."

"I've got four paws. Which are which?"

"To pause means to stop," said Emma. "But let's move on. Have you ever sung, Freddie?"

"Sure," he said. "Us cats used to hang around the ledge at night meowing our heads off. That was in my kitten days."

"Caterwauling is not singing," Emma explained. "You must learn words. You'll have to start listening to records."

"The old lady plays the phonograph when she cleans," said Freddie. "She's got a bunch of corny old numbers. I always take a nap when she puts them on."

"Well start listening," said Emma. "Tomorrow, I want you to sing me a song."

That afternoon, Mrs. Bitterman put on her favorite old record as she dusted the apartment. Freddie sat by the phonograph, listening. The old lady played the song three times, but he still hadn't learned all the lyrics. Then Mrs. Bitterman went to the kitchen to brew tea. Freddie picked up the needle and replaced it at the beginning of the record. He played it three more times. The fourth time he sang along, trying hard to match the melody.

When Mrs. Bitterman came to the doorway, her teacup dropped to the floor. It was Freddie, not Herbert, tinkering with the phonograph! "Herbert!" she shouted, "come quick. Now Freddie's *singing!*"

Freddie quickly scampered under the sofa. Only his tail was visible when Mr. Bitterman entered.

"I'm not imagining things," Mrs. Bitterman insisted. "I *heard* it. He put the record on himself."

"So now he sings?" sighed Mr. Bitterman, picking up the broken china. "So maybe he wants to be in the show business?"

"Very funny, Herbert," grumbled his wife.

The next day, Freddie sang his song for Emma. He included in his performance a clever soft-shoe dance around the fire escape. Unfortunately, his paddies kept getting stuck between the rungs. But the song sounded great:

A B C D E F G H . . .
I got a gal in Kalamazoo.
Don't want to boast
But I know she's the toast
Of Kalamazoo.
Going to Michigan
To see the sweetest gal
In Kalamazoo—zoo—zoo!

"Why, that's lovely," Emma cooed. "You learned a song and practiced your alphabet, too."

"It'd be better with a straw hat," said Freddie, puffing.

"That reminds me," said Emma. "Maude's got a surprise for you. Come up and I'll show you."

Freddie followed Emma up the fire escape to her roost. Maude was fluttering around excitedly, putting finishing touches on her display.

"What do you think?" she asked eagerly. "Isn't it super?"

Freddie looked around. Lying along the ledge was a collection of clothing and jewelry. There were holey socks, torn stockings, bits of net and lace, torn silk scarves and ties, unmatched gloves, one fuzzy slipper, broken bracelets, a ripped pajama top, three earrings, a baby's bib and a beat-up beach hat with dusty plastic flowers.

"This all for me?" asked Freddie.

"They're your costumes," Maude explained proudly. "We found them in the trash. Been collecting them for days."

"In Shakespeare's day," said Emma. "Men played all the roles. Even the ladies."

"But how'd you manage?"

"We all helped," Emma cooed. "Even Clarence."

"That's right," he said from the corner. "Roscoe and me almost broke our beaks on that slipper. It took an hour to drag it up here."

"Now you can dress up and be whoever you like," said Maude.

"This hat's terrific," said Freddie, popping it on his head. He shuffled across the ledge, singing his song:

> *A B C D E F G H . . .*
> *I got a gal*
> *In Kalamazoo.*
> *Don't want to boast*
> *But I know she's the toast*
> *Of Kalamazoo—zoo—zoo*

"Is *that* what Em's been teaching you?" asked Clarence.

"I learned it myself," said Freddie proudly. "Now, all I need's a cane."

"Let's find a big branch in the park," chirped Maude.

"Not now, dear," said Emma. "We must finish our

lesson. It's the most important one. Freddie, it's time for you to choose your character. You must pick someone you know and try to behave just like them."

"But who should I pick?"

"*Any*one."

Freddie thought a minute. "I know," he said. "Miss Lucy. I could act like her real easy. All that phony-baloney talk and snootiness. What a put-on." Freddie sat up, daintily poking out his right paw. "Only the best," he mimicked in a screechy-scratchy voice. "Good gracious, I smell soot!"

"That's funny," Maude giggled.

"Very good," said Emma. "Now, you must do it for Miss Lucy."

"But she *hates* me," Freddie argued. "She almost kicked me out last time. I never want to see her again."

"But you must," said Emma. "Miss Lucy hates you as Freddie. Convince her you've reformed and become just like her. That will prove you can play a character."

"Okay, I'll try," said Freddie. "But it ain't gonna be easy!"

Trial Run

Getting to see Miss Lucy wasn't easy, either. She never came near the fire escape or sat by the window. But Freddie devised a plan. He'd slip through Miss Iver's kitchen window and sneak into Miss Lucy's bedroom.   .

Later that night, Emma flew down to the third floor ledge as Freddie crawled down the fire escape.

"I'll stay here and observe your performance," she whispered. "Good luck."

"You mean break a leg, dont'cha, Em?"

Emma smiled and nodded. Cautiously, Freddie glanced around the kitchen to be sure Miss Ivers wasn't baking another batch of muffins. Empty. He tiptoed through the hall. The bathroom door was shut. He heard the sound of running water. Perfect timing. With Miss Ivers safely tucked in the tub, he'd have plenty of time to con—er, *persuade* Miss Lucy.

As Freddie reached her doorway, he closed his eyes to summon up all the knowledge he'd learned over the weeks. Nervously, he scratched outside Miss Lucy's door.

"Who is it?"

"'Tis me!" said Freddie in his most cultured, Shakespearian tone.

"Tissie? Don't know any Tissie. Go away, I'm napping."

Freddie poked the door open with his paw, then stuck his head inside. "Having your beauty sleep, no doubt?"

Miss Lucy was resting on a pile of pillows by the window seat. "Oh, it's *you*," she said in disgust. "Has Mrs. Bitterman dragged you down again? I hoped I'd seen the last of you."

"I'm not with my old lad—Mrs. Bitterman," he

said, gliding across the room. "I've come by myself."

"Then leave by yourself," snapped the Persian, fluffing her tail.

Freddie glanced out the window. Emma was seated on the sill. He pointed to Miss Lucy then shook his head back and forth. The plan wasn't working. Emma nodded insistently, signaling Freddie to keep trying.

Miss Lucy glanced up from her pillows, noticing Freddie's peculiar shakey movements. "What's the matter?" she asked, as Freddie's head quivered. "Why are you shaking? Whatever you've got, I hope it's not contagious."

Freddie shook his head harder, gesturing toward the window. But Emma continued nodding hers. Then suddenly, Freddie got a brainstorm. He knew how to impress the old Persian. Accidentally, he'd hit upon her favorite topic of conversation—illness. Miss Lucy loved discussing disease. "I'm very well," he said, suddenly inspired. "It's just my allergy acting up again."

"That's strange," she said sarcastically. "I never knew common cats had allergies; they're only for delicate creatures like myself. You ruffian types are too insensitive to be sick."

"I have many allergies," said Freddie proudly. "They run in the family. My mother was allergic to everything."

"Including you, no doubt," Miss Lucy yawned. "Just what are you allergic to?"

Freddie thought back to all the things Miss Lucy had mentioned—hairs, dust, dirt, flowers. He'd have to make up something impressive. "Pine needles," he said.

"Pine needles? But there are no pine trees on Riverside Drive."

"That's why I live here," he snapped. "Checked out the neighborhood years ago. But someone must've brought home a pine pillow from vacation. I'm beginning to get the shakes again."

"What an unusual allergy," said Miss Lucy, obviously impressed. "Tell me, what do you do at Christmas time?"

"What do you mean?"

"Well," she said suspiciously, "the building's filled with pine trees at Christmas."

"Oh, yes," said Freddie, "that's when the Bitterman's send me away. You've never seen me on Christmas, have you?"

"No," she said thoughtfully. "I never have."

"Oh, it's a horrible sight," Freddie continued. "The old folks, poor things, can't stand it. They ship me to—uh—a clinic in Florida. Allergies Anonymous. That's where cats with difficult problems go."

"I've never heard of it," said Miss Lucy, her ears standing on point. "I wonder why Miss Ivers never sent *me*."

"Perhaps you don't qualify," said Freddie haughtily. "Any cat can sneeze from dust; that's nothing special. But you should see me when *I* have an attack. It's unbelieveable!"

"Tell me about it," she said eagerly.

"Well," said Freddie, inching closer, "first, my eyes get as big as melons. Then my tongue turns brown and hangs out like a piece of wet liver. Next, my paddies swell up to the size of bowling balls."

"How marvelous!" said Miss Lucy. "You must be a classic case."

"Oh, I am. I appear in all the medical books. Pine-itus, it's called. I've got one of the worst cases on record."

"Who's your doctor?" she asked. "I've been in many medical waiting rooms, but I've never heard of your disease."

"Stanawhosky," said Freddie. "He's the master. Fifty dollars a visit, but it's worth it. Only the best, you know."

"Miss Ivers takes me to Dr. Benson on Fifth Avenue."

"Benson's a good man," said Freddie casually, "for little things like hangnails and fur balls. But someone like me needs a *specialist*."

"I imagine so," she admitted. "But I've some rather classic allergies myself. I simply can't go near rose petals."

"What's in a name," quoted Freddie, remembering his Shakespeare. "That which we call a rose by any other name would smell as sweet."

"Perhaps," said Miss Lucy. "But they *still* itch my eyes. Dr. Benson's given me some pills, but they don't seem to work."

"Benson's a good man," Freddie repeated. "But he's not the *best*. I've got pills Doc Stanawhosky gave me that'll put hair on your chest."

Miss Lucy glanced down at herself. "My chest seems fine," she said. "But my tail could use a bit of fluffing out. I don't suppose you have any extra, do you, Freddie dear?"

"Well, I don't know," he said. "They're made up just for me. I can't pass them out to just anybody"

"*I'm* not just anybody!" she snapped.

"That's true," said Freddie. No sense offending the old girl after all his work. "I guess I could give you a few."

"How sweet," she purred. "Why not run upstairs and get them? We'll continue chatting when you return."

Reluctantly, Freddie agreed. He tippy-toed out the

kitchen window, onto the fire escape where Emma was waiting. "How am I doin?" he asked.

"Wonderfully," she whispered, "but you have no pills for Miss Lucy, have you?"

"Not yet," he said. "But I better find some fast."

Freddie entered the apartment, slowly padding past the bedroom where the old folks were watching TV. Jumping on the kitchen sink, he glanced through the cupboard. *What* could he bring Miss Lucy? Mr. Bitterman's malt tablets might pass for pills. No, there was something better. Pussy Pellet Balls! Miss Lucy was such a fusspot, she'd never *seen* cat food. Freddie smiled and grabbed a pawful. He dashed from the apartment, back into Miss Lucy's air-conditioned room. "Here you are," he said, placing the brown balls on her rug. "Help yourself."

Miss Lucy looked down. "What strange pills," she said. She sniffed them suspiciously. "Are you sure they work?"

"A dollar apiece," said Freddie, popping one into his mouth. "Only the best. I feel better already."

"You have stopped shaking," Miss Lucy noticed.

"Cures the shakes every time. Go on, try them."

Cautiously, Miss Lucy placed a pellet in her mouth and began to chew. "Quite a nutty flavor," she said. "Most unusual."

"Your tail looks better already, Loo," said Freddie.

"Do you think so?" she purred, glancing down at

it. "It's always been my finest feature." She leaned over and gobbled up the remainder of the pellets. When finished, she opened her mouth in a wide yawn, curled up into a ball and closed her eyes. "I'm feeling better already," she said sleepily. "It pays to buy the best."

"Sure does," Freddie agreed. "I'd better be going now, Loo. Maybe I'll stop by again, to check on how you're doing. We allergic cats must stick together, you know."

"That's true," yawned Miss Lucy. "When you stop by, bring more of those delicious pills."

"Will do," said Freddie. "Now get your beauty sleep. You need it."

"I do, I do," said the Persian, drifting off to sleep.

Once certain the cat was asleep, Freddie kicked up his paws, twirled around the room with pleasure, then dashed out the door and into the kitchen. He heard Miss Iver's floppy slippers padding through the hallway just as he jumped back onto the fire escape.

"How'd I do, Em?" he asked excitedly.

"You were *marvelous*," cooed Emma with delight. "Simply marvelous."

"I sure had the old girl impressed, didn't I?"

"Indeed you did," Emma giggled. "One of the finest performances I've ever seen."

"Pretty terrific, eh? How'd you like that allergy junk? And those pineitus pills?"

"All perfect," said Emma. "You analyzed your character, then became just like her. That's true acting."

"Yeah," sighed Freddie. He lay on his back and stared up at the stars. "One thing bothers me, though," he said. "I didn't know being an actor meant telling so many lies."

"Those weren't lies. That was a *performance*. You were playing a part—being a character. And you did it most convincingly. In fact, you made Miss Lucy feel good. She went to sleep, thinking she was more beautiful than ever. That's better than fighting with her."

"That's right," said Freddie. "It's the first time she didn't call me Scarface."

"You not only gave a fine performance," said Emma. "You settled an old quarrel. An excellent night's work."

"Yeah," said Freddie, staring at the stars, "you're right." Yet, he still felt a strange, empty sensation. Something was missing. The applause! All the actors in New Jersey got applause.

Sensing his need, Emma began fluttering above the windowsill. "Bravo!" she shouted. "Take a bow!"

Freddie bowed his head. "Thanks, Em." He grinned.

As Emma fluttered back to her sill, she bumped

her head against the windowpane. "Goodness," she sighed, "it's gotten dark."

"It's not the dark," said Freddie with concern. "It's your eyes. They've been bothering you, haven't they?"

"Perhaps," she admitted. "Just a bit."

"That's my fault," said Freddie. "You've been staying up late reading on account of me."

"Oh, but I've loved it," she said. "Every minute. I hate to have it end."

"End?"

"Yes, Freddie," she said sadly. "Tonight was your last lesson. I've taught you all I know. You're ready to go into the world and become a star."

"No kidding! I really did it? But wait a minute," he added. "That means you and me won't be having classes no more."

"I'm afraid not. I've taught you everything."

"Oh," he said haltingly. "Well, you've sure been a swell teacher."

"And you've been a superior pupil."

"I have a present for ya, Em. I wasn't sure when to give it. But I guess this is the time."

"A present?"

"It's upstairs. Hop on my back. I'll take you there."

Emma climbed onto Freddie's back, perching her claws inside his soft fur. When they reached the Bitterman's ledge, Freddie let Emma down. Then he bounced through the window. "Wait here," he said. "I'll get it." He returned with something in his mouth and placed it on the fire escape. "I guess teachers are supposed to get apples, but this is better."

"What is it?" asked Emma, peering through the dim light.

"Eyeglasses." Freddie picked them up and held them close to Emma's face. One pane was broken but the other was perfect. Emma stared through it. Instantly, Freddie's shining green eyes doubled in size. "How marvelous!" she chirped. "It magnifies."

"They're the old man's reading glasses. He dropped 'em one night when he saw me dance. Bumped right into the wall. I've been saving them for ya, Em."

"How sweet, Freddie. But I couldn't take your old man—Mr. Bitterman's glasses."

"He's got another pair. Besides, you need 'em. I tied a string around 'em, see? You can hang it on your neck. Take 'em, Em, it's my way to say thanks."

Freddie placed the string in his mouth and dropped it over Emma's neck. She glanced at the glass as it caught the moonlight. "It's the loveliest gift I've ever received," she said, choked with pride. "I'll wear them always."

"Ya better," he said, sniffing slightly. "Before ya

get cross-eyed. Can't have no cross-eyed birds bumping around."

"No indeed," she smiled, "that wouldn't do."

"Well, I'll see ya to your ledge," said Freddie, his voice quivering. "Good-bye. And thanks for everything."

"Wait," said Emma. "We can't say good-bye. Not now."

"My lessons are over, Em. I'm going out into the show business."

"True," she said, "you're not a student any more. But you're still not a star. You'll have to audition and rehearse. You must select a play and write a resume. You'll have to find a theater to perform in. You can't act on the fire escape."

"Gosh, I hadn't thought of that stuff. Sounds like a lot of work. Don't know if I can do it."

"You *can't*," said Emma. "Not alone. You'll need *my* help."

"But you've already taught me all you know."

"Then I'll have to learn more," she said decisively. "I'll start in the morning. With your talent and my glasses, nothing can stop us."

"Gee, Em." Freddie purred. "You're some terrific bird!"

Freddie's
Past Is Revealed

Next morning, wearing her new glasses, Emma went
up to her office. Eagerly, she checked through her
Culture file, which listed museums and libraries.
Emma'd been satisfied with the 42nd Street library,
but now she had to specialize. She found the address
of Lincoln Center Library for the Performing Arts,
then flew off to visit it.

Tall buildings with wide glass windows overlooked

a shooting fountain set in the center of a plaza. The library building was at the rear of the complex. Hopping along a ledge at the windows, she glanced over the shoulders of people reading inside. One boy was reading about John Barrymore, another about Edwin Booth. A young man was taking notes on the Bolshoi Ballet. One woman browsed through *Sex and Violence in Cinema* and another read *The Performance of Puppetry*. Emma learned a lot, but none of it helped Freddie.

After two hours, she took a lunch break. When she returned to the sill, she noticed a man reading by a corner table. The book was called *The City's Theaters*, a history of the theater as it moved uptown from Bowling Green to Times Square. Then he opened another, *Famous New York Theaters*, filled with pictures, addresses and famous performances. Just what Emma needed! Unfortunately, after a while the man closed the book and checked it out of the library. Sadly, Emma watched him tuck the information under his arm and leave the building.

But as he walked across the plaza, several loose pages slipped unnoticed from the binding. Caught in a gust of wind, they circled through the air, landing on the ledge beside Emma, a personal gift from the Fates. Happily, she tucked them into her beak and flew home.

Freddie was taking his sunbath when Emma returned. She dropped the papers beside him. "Hi, Em," he said drowsily. "What's up?"

"I've learned all about theaters," she explained. "In the suburbs and in the country there are summer stock and tent theaters like the one you saw in New Jersey. In the city, there are small theaters way downtown called Off-Broadway houses; and even smaller ones in churches and lofts called Off-Off-Broadway. But the biggest and most famous are those *on* Broadway. The most famous actors in the world work there. That's where *you* belong, Freddie."

"*Broadway?*" gasped Freddie nervously. "Me go to *Broadway?* No way, Em. Can't catch me dead up there!"

"But Freddie, I don't understand."

"Listen, Em, Broadway's two blocks from here, and I know all about it. The old folks used to walk me on a leash, right up 99th Street. I'm *never* going back. Know what's up there, Em? People pushing and shoving, junk in the streets. It's crawling with weirdos. Broadway Crazies, I call 'em. One nutty guy used to talk into his shoe. And some crazy lady wore a straw hat with a veil and scarf shoved up her nose. She'd hit people with her purse and shout, '*Salvation!*' Worst of all, no one paid attention. Scared me half to death."

"That's not the Broadway I mean," said Emma. "There's a bigger, far more famous section downtown called Times Square." Emma began reciting the facts she'd memorized that afternoon. "This section consists of the blocks from 38th to 59th Street, between Sixth and Eighth Avenues, mainly east and west from 43rd to 52nd Street. In 1895, electric street lighting reached 42nd Street, signaling the birth of 'The Great White Way,' which Broadway has been known as ever since. In 1967, the city declared Times Square the official Theater District. The three Shubert brothers built many theaters in the area at the turn of the century. Therefore, the district is often referred to as Shubert Alley."

"Yeah, yeah," said Freddie impatiently, "but what about the Broadway Crazies? What did ya learn about *them*?"

"Not a thing," said Emma. "They weren't mentioned."

"No Broadway Crazies? Do ya suppose they're gone?"

"Perhaps," she said. "Besides, they don't concern us. Right now, we must select the proper theater for your debut."

"My what?"

"Debut," she repeated. "Dā-bu as pronounced in the original French; or dé-boo if you prefer the Brit-

ish. It means to make your first appearance on stage;
the beginning of your professional career."

"Oh yeah. My day-boo."

"Now here's a list of theaters," said Emma, pointing a claw. This is the Winthrop Ames on 44th Street.
Their opening production was on March 12, 1912.
The name of the play was *The Pigeon*. But that won't
do. It's been torn down. Perhaps this one," she continued, turning the page. "The Longacre Theatre,
220 west 48th Street, which opened in 1913. A play
called *Rhinoceros* had a successful run there in 1961."

As Emma continued, Freddie stretched out on the
fire escape. He couldn't shake the image of the Broadway Crazies.

"Here's a possibility," Emma chirped. "This theater housed the prize-winning play of 1954, *Cat on a
Hot Tin Roof*. And that's not all," she added. "It's
opening play in February 5, 1917 was called *Canary
Cottage*; a musical. They don't say who played the
canary, but Trixie Friganza played the fat cook." She
pushed the paper toward Freddie. "Two productions
starring animals. And a handsome building. The address is perfect, 217 west 45th Street, in the heart of
the theater district, Shubert Alley."

Freddie glanced down at the page. Suddenly, his
eyes widened and a chill of recognition ran through
his body. Vague memories of kittenhood came flow-

ing back. "That's it," he shouted, pointing at the photograph. "That's the one."

"I'm glad you agree," said Emma. "A debut is an important occasion. We wouldn't want to make a mistake."

"No, Em," he said excitedly. "Ya don't understand. That's the place where I was *born*!"

"Not really!" said Emma. "Are you certain?"

"I couldn't forget it in a million years," he shouted. "That big white door; the alley to the side. That's it, I tell ya. What's it called?"

Eagerly, Emma glanced at the name. "The Morosco," she said solemnly. "The Morosco Theatre!"

"I told ya!" said Freddie triumphantly. "That's me, Em. Frederick Morosco Bitterman. I never knew what my middle name meant before, but now I do. The old folks named me after the theater where I was born."

"Oh Freddie," said Emma. "Do you know what this means? You're not an alley cat, after all. You're a *Shubert Alley* cat!"

Freddie Prepares
for Broadway

The next day, while reading through the *New York Times*, Emma discovered more exciting news. The Morosco Theatre was preparing a revival of *Cat on a Hot Tin Roof*. She and Freddie agreed he should audition for the lead. Of course, he'd need an audition piece.

Luckily, Emma had parts of *Richard II* tucked in

her files. They selected a scene and for five nights, snuck up to the penthouse to rehearse. Under Mr. Olson's lamplight, they repeated the lines over and over. But it wasn't easy. Shakespeare was really hard to understand.

"I don't figure it," whispered Freddie one evening. (They always spoke softly, for fear of disturbing Mr. Olson.) "Old King Richard says, 'Give me the glass and therein will I read.' That don't make sense. How can ya read in a mirror? Then he says, 'A brittle glory shineth in this face.' What's that mean, peanut brittle? Ya figure he smeared peanut brittle on his face?"

"I don't know, Freddie," Emma whispered. "Perhaps it's enough to know the words without the meaning."

"Maybe so," he agreed.

"What's all the chattering?" squeaked Clarence, fluttering onto the roof.

"Sshh," Emma cautioned. "We're rehearsing."

"But, Em, it's almost midnight. Can't this wait till morning?"

"It cannot, she insisted. Freddie's got tons of work before he makes his debut.

"His what?"

"Debut," Emma repeated. "Dā-bu as pronounced in the original French, or dé-boo if you prefer the British."

"You know what I'd prefer," Clarence grumbled. "A good night's sleep!" He hopped along the ledge, stumbling over a rock that lay across one of Emma's files. "What've you got up here?" he snapped, "land mines? What is this stuff?"

"Sshh," she whispered. "They're my files."

"Sure are piles," he shouted. "Of junk! A regular fire hazard."

Freddie continued reciting his lines. "For there it is," he quoted, "crackt in a hundred shivers"

"Cracked is right," Clarence snapped. "You're *both* cracked. Why'd I let you start this nonsense? I haven't had a decent night's sleep since . . ."

Suddenly, Clarence heard a sound. Mr. Olson was coming. His shadowy figure passed by the window. He leaned out and peered across the rooftop. Freddie, Emma and Clarence huddled in silence. Mr. Olson slammed the window shut, then pulled the shade.

"I told you not to chatter," Emma scolded. "Now we've lost the light."

"That's not all you've lost," Clarence grumbled.

"Listen guys," said Freddie diplomatically. "Wanna come to my place for a midnight snack? The old folks leave out lots of stuff."

"Got any crackers?" asked Clarence.

"Even better. Miss Ivers was up this morning. There's a closetful of corn muffins."

"Clarence loves corn muffins, don't you dear?"

"They're not bad," he admitted. "But they're better with jelly."

The corn muffins, even minus jelly, had a soothing effect on Clarence. While the old folks slept, Freddie and his guests sat on the Bitterman's kitchen sill, nibbling their nightcap. When filled to the beak, Clarence agreed to be patient awhile longer. To insure his good humor, Freddie promised to bring him muffins while the supply lasted. It was bribery, but Emma said nothing. If corn muffins could save her marriage, she'd accept them gratefully.

Freddie rehearsed his part three more nights, until he'd finally memorized it. Then it was time to prepare a résumé. "All good actors need one," Emma explained. "It's a list of all the parts you've played."

"I ain't played any parts yet," said Freddie.

"Yes you have," said Emma. "We'll go up to the penthouse later and type it out."

That night at eleven o'clock, Mr. Olson made himself hot chocolate, then took his usual thirty-minute nap.

"Now's our chance," Emma whispered, peeking through his window. "He's even left a clean page in the machine."

Freddie tippy-toed through the window, and Emma fluttered toward the typewriter. "I'll start dictating," she whispered. Freddie poked at the keys Emma pointed to. Within twenty minutes, the résumé was complete. "Excellent," said Emma, reading it aloud:

NAME: Frederick Morosco Bitterman
AGE: Six Big Ones
ADDRESS: Bitterman Home, Riverside Drive
BACKGROUND: Theater folks from Shubert Alley
EDUCATION: Studied with Stanislavski
PREVIOUS ROLES: 1. Co-starred with Miss Lucy in a
                   play called *Pussy Pellets*
                2. Understudied all the parts in New
                   Jersey

"Gee, those lies sound great," Freddie grinned. "*I'd* hire me."

"They're not lies," Emma insisted. "You *did* act with Miss Lucy. And you understudied all summer. You sat under that theater tent, learning all the parts, didn't you?"

"Yeah."

"Well, if you studied under the tent, you understudied."

"That's right," said Freddie, laughing.

Suddenly, Mr. Olson snorted under his breath. He rolled over on the sofa and raised his head.

"He's waking up," Emma whispered.

Freddie quickly ripped the page from the typewriter with his teeth. Emma hopped on his back and they bounced out the open window.

Freddie's Debut

The big day finally arrived. Excited twitters sprang up along the 99th Street ledge. Resident sparrows and pigeons passed the word from one dovecote to another. "Freddie's ready," they chattered. "He's going downtown today."

"Has Emma finally hatched that plot of hers?" grumbled Sanford Pigeon. "Maybe now we can get some rest."

"Bet Clarence is glad it's over," cried Roscoe. "Now we can celebrate."

"I certainly wish them luck," cooed Monica Pigeon. "Poor Emma deserves it. She's worked her beak to the bone for that cat. Practically gone blind, too!"

At Emma's ledge, she and Freddie fussed over last-minute details.

"Should I wear my straw hat?" he asked nervously.

"Oh, do," said Emma. "You want to be noticed. Other cats may be auditioning, too. It makes you look distinctive."

"Stinktive is right." Clarence laughed. "You look like a screwball."

"Oh, he's cute," said Maude. "But you need a little powder, Freddie. Just a touch on the nose." She slapped him in the face with a large pink puff she'd found in the alley.

"And carry your pencil," said Willie, sticking it in Freddie's mouth. "It makes you look *educated*. Educated cats get better jobs."

"And don't forget your résumé," said Emma, tucking that in his mouth, too. "And you'll need a tie," she added, slipping a torn red one over his neck. She sat back and looked at him. "Yes," she nodded, "that's perfect. I think we're ready."

"Good luck," chirped Maude as Freddie and Emma descended the fire escape stairs.

"Good luck," twittered the sparrows and pigeons hanging from the ledge. "Come back a star."

"Or don't come back at all," mumbled Sanford Pigeon.

When they got to the sidewalk, Freddie looked up and waved a paw in fond farewell. Then he and Emma hurried down the block.

As Freddie walked along the crowded streets, he didn't notice the throngs of shoppers. He hardly heard the blasting sounds of truck and automobile horns. He was too excited, too nervous to notice anything. Emma flew above him, guiding his way downtown.

After half an hour, they arrived at 45th Street. Almost instinctively, Freddie turned the corner toward the Morosco Theater. There, he saw the darkened alley where he'd spent his kittenhood. It filled him with a strange nostalgia. Home again! Proudly, he marched toward the stage entrance. But the door was locked and bolted.

"I can't understand it," said Emma. "The actors' entrance should be open. Wait here, while I check the main door."

Emma fluttered toward the front of the building. Outside, the theater marquee read CAT ON A HOT TIN ROOF. There was a poster by the doorway:

OPENING NIGHT 8 O'CLOCK
Sold Out!
Ella Stoddard repeats her award-winning role as
MAGGIE THE CAT

Oh no! Freddie was too late. The part had already been cast. And it had gone to a *female*. With leaden wings, Emma flew back to tell her friend the depressing news. "It's too late," she said sadly. "The play opens tonight. They already have a star."

Freddie was silent. Sitting alone in the alley of his old home had filled him with self-confidence.

"Didn't you hear me?" Emma repeated. "We're too late."

"It's never too late," he said. "*You* taught me that."

"But this is different, Freddie. And it's my fault. I've ruined your big chance."

"Hold it, Em. No one's gonna spoil *my* chance. So they've got a star. But maybe he's no good. Or maybe he won't show up."

"*She*," said Emma, revealing the last bit of bad news. "They cast a female in the part."

"Oh well," he said. "Maybe *she* won't show up. Or maybe they need some chorus cats. There'll be a spot for me somewhere, you'll see."

"But the show doesn't start until eight o'clock," Emma argued. "I can't wait. I promised Clarence never to fly at night."

"You can leave, Em. I'll be okay."

"But can you manage without me?" she asked. Emma hated to miss Freddie's "day-boo," after all her hard work.

"I know my part real good," he said, straightening his tie. He began to recite:

> *A brittle glory shineth in this face;*
> *As brittle as the glory is the face;*
> *For there it is, crackt in a hundred shivers.*
> *Mark silent king, the moral of this sport,*
> *How soon my sorrow hath destroy'd my face.*

Freddie took a deep bow, careful not to knock his hat off. "See, Em," he smiled. "I know every word. I'm gonna be fine."

"Well, if you're sure. But don't forget all I've taught you. When you walk on stage, hold your head high."

"Right."

"Speak your lines clearly and distinctly. Enunciate."

"You've got it, Em."

"And don't let the audience scare you. The finest actors have stage fright."

"Quit worrying. I'm gonna be okay."

"Perhaps we should run through your speech again. It never . . ."

"Bye-bye, Em," said Freddie, waving his paw. "I'll stop by your ledge tonight and tell ya everything."

Emma, unable to think of one more helpful hint, slowly fluttered away. Freddie looked up and smiled. She had one last glimpse at her prize pupil.

When Emma arrived back at the ledge, all the birds clustered around, surprised to see her home so soon.

"How was it?" asked Willie.

"How'd it go?" chirped Clarence.

"You back already?" snapped Sanford.

"Where's Freddie?" asked Roscoe.

"Is he a star yet?" tweeted Maude.

"Not exactly," said Emma. "But everything's going to be fine. Freddie says so."

The birds stared in confusion. But Emma refused to say another word. "Let's talk about it later," she said, sighing. "Much later."

Freddie waited in the alleyway as the afternoon sun set. An autumn chill brushed along the street. Darkness fell. Suddenly, the sidewalk brightened with a blaze of neon. Lights from theater marquees switched on along the avenue.

Slowly, the Morosco Theater stirred with signs of life. The backstage entrance was unlocked and footsteps rushed along the stairs. Voices buzzed. People gathered beside the box office entrance. The theater aisles, dark and silent moments before, lit up. Stage-hands rushed back and forth, busily checking lights and sets.

Cautiously, Freddie padded down the corridor of EXIT 11, which led inside. The theater was so huge; not at all like the tent in New Jersey. There were rows of plush red seats and a large balcony. Around the upper side walls, small booths seemed to float in midair. Large crystal chandeliers twinkled from the ceiling and heavy beige draperies hung on the walls.

As the audience arrived, Freddie snuck behind a pillar near the corner wall. From here, he could jump on stage, if the star cat didn't show up. Once the audience was seated, the lights dimmed and the velvet curtains parted. The play had begun.

Freddie watched in silence, waiting for the cats to come on. But none appeared, not even a kitten; just a woman called Maggie the cat. By the time the third act had begun, Freddie had figured out the awful truth. There were no animals in the play! Just people. They didn't need a cat after all.

There Freddie sat, still eager to perform. But no one knew. No one *cared*. As the curtain closed on the final act, waves of applause filled the theater. The actors smiled and took their bows. Suddenly, Freddie decided to seize that moment to make himself known. He pounced onto the stage, startling the cast.

The audience was surprised, too. They muttered among themselves and stared at the intruder. Freddie could feel their eyes piercing through him. Watching. Waiting. It made him so nervous, he forgot everything. Instantly, all the lessons he'd learned went rushing through his head at once. His acting, singing and dancing got mushed up with his diction and Shakespeare.

Freddie dropped his résumé onto the stage. He cleared his throat, shook his paws and straightened his hat. Then he began to dance. At first, he did a graceful pirouette. But then he spun around, bumping into the table of the set. He quickly switched into his sand dance. But there wasn't any sand. Nervously, he began his soft-shoe number and started singing:

> *A B C D E F G H*
> *Peanut brittle on your face*
> *She's crackt in shivers*
> *But she still makes toast*
> *In Kalamazoo—zoo—zoo*

Oh dear, that didn't sound right! Anxiously, Freddie recited the one Shakespearean line he couldn't forget: "Good king, great king, and yet, not greatly good." For his finale, he did three tumbles across the stage. Once again, he bumped into the table, squashing his hat down over his eyes.

The audience stared. They barely believed what

they saw. But suddenly, they all began laughing and applauding. Even the actors! Cameras began to click, and people started shouting.

"What a riot," laughed one actor.

"A great publicity stunt," called someone from the audience.

"Terrific," yelled a woman in the first row. "Where'd they find that cat?"

"I bet this was the producer's idea," shouted an old man, laughing.

Freddie fixed his hat, grinned and bowed. He'd messed everything up, but they'd liked him. He was a hit! Then, just as Freddie was taking his third curtain call, a man shouted from the balcony, "Hold that cat! I want that cat!"

"I'll catch him," yelled someone, running down the aisle.

Within moments, half the audience jumped to their feet. Freddie panicked as he saw them all stamping toward the stage. People rushed around, bumping into one another, acting *crazy*. Freddie pounced to the ground and dashed toward the exit. All that remained on stage was his rolled-up résumé, still moist with tooth marks. The young man who'd rushed from the balcony picked it up and read it. "This is fantastic," he screamed. "I've just got to have that cat!"

It was after midnight when Freddie arrived back at the ledge. Emma was still awake, waiting to hear the news. Freddie told her how wonderful the evening had been. He was a success. He was marvelous! *Brilliant!* Of course, he didn't mention messing everything up. That wasn't important. What mattered was that the audience *loved* him.

"I'm so proud of you," Emma cooed. "So, you got the part."

"Not exactly," said Freddie. He hadn't told Emma there were no cats in the play. He didn't mention the screwball who'd shouted from the balcony. Those details could wait until morning. For now, he stretched out and looked up at the stars. They twinkled down just for him, while the sound of applause still buzzed in his ears.

Freddie Returns
to Broadway

"I don't believe it!" shouted Emma the next morning, after Freddie had revealed all. "Why would people title plays for animals if animals aren't in them?"

"They're peculiar," Freddie explained. "First, that audience was applauding me; then it started to *stampede*. I bet that guy in the balcony was a Broadway Crazy."

"What did he shout at you, Freddie?"

"When I finished my speech, he yelled 'Hold that cat! I've gotta have that cat!' That's when I made a dash for the door."

"Perhaps he was the playwright," said Emma. "Or the producer."

"Well, I don't know why he got so mad. Everyone *loved* me. Even the actors."

"That's it!" said Emma. "He *was* the producer. He wanted to offer you the lead. He probably cast a human because they couldn't find a talented cat."

"Someone *did* mention a producer," Freddie remembered. "Just before the attack."

"I knew I was right," twittered Emma excitedly, just as Roscoe fluttered by the fire escape. "Hi guys," he chirped between hiccups. "I've been sent to get the verdict. Is Freddie a flop or a star?"

"Half and half," said Freddie.

"Oh yeah?" giggled Roscoe, hiccuping again. "Does that mean you're a floppy star or a star flop?"

"What's the matter with you?" asked Emma. "You seem quite giddy."

"Up late celebrating," he explained. "Me and Clarence. Guess we had one bun too many."

"And where is Clarence now?" asked Emma coolly. "Still sleeping it off, no doubt."

"Don't be hard on him," said Roscoe. "He's so glad this non—uh—studying is over. It's not easy watching a star get born. Harder than watching eggs hatch. Speaking of that, Em, your kids slept over at Monica's place. They're itching to know the details. Old Sanford was taking bets all night. He got a few votes for success, but most of the guys figured Freddie'd be a washout."

"Is that so," said Emma indignantly.

"Not me, ya understand. But you've gotta admit the whole thing's pretty nutty."

"It may seem nutty to a *sparrow*, but the Broadway audience thought Freddie was fantastic. They gave him a standing ovation last night."

"No kidding," said Roscoe.

"Absolutely. Dozens of curtain calls. Broadway's newest shining star."

"Is that right?" said Roscoe. "You were a big deal, huh, Freddie?"

"Well," he answered humbly, "I guess."

"Of course he was," said Emma. "Though it shouldn't surprise you. He had an excellent teacher!"

"Sure, but all those curtain calls," said Roscoe. "Did they really flip out like that?"

"Freddie's too modest to admit it," Emma continued, "but he was a sensation. In fact, they want him for the *lead*."

"They do?" said Roscoe.

"They *do*?" asked Freddie.

"We're meeting with the producer this afternoon," said Emma.

"You are?" said Roscoe.

"We *are*?" asked Freddie.

"We will be," Emma replied. "Today is Wednesday, matinee day. I can fly downtown with you."

"How's about the old folks?" he asked. "They'll miss me if I'm gone."

"We'll be back by dinner," said Emma. "Now run inside and get your beach hat. It's your good luck charm."

"Hold it," said Roscoe, his head spinning. "Who's this producer? When did all this happen?"

"It hasn't," said Emma. "Not yet. But it will!"

"What am I gonna tell Clarence when he wakes up? You know how grumpy he gets when you fly the coop."

"Tell him I'll be busy all afternoon. Negotiating."

"Go-she-what?"

"Just tell 'em we're gone," said Freddie, throwing on his hat.

Roscoe leaned over the ledge as Freddie and Emma disappeared up 99th Street. "Clarence isn't gonna like this," he groaned. "Not one bit!"

With Emma on his back, Freddie led the way through the backstage entrance of the Morosco Theater. The curtain was open, and one spotlight shone down on the deserted set.

"It's so big," Emma cooed. "Was it hard performing for so many people?"

"A snap," said Freddie, jumping on stage. "I had 'em in my paws the whole time."

Emma fluttered about the stage, then settled on the edge of the sofa. "Please show me what you did, Freddie. I'd love to see."

"First, I gave 'em the ballet business," he explained, turning on tippy-toe. "Then into my shoft-shoe routine, followed by my show-stopping Kalamazoo number."

"But what about Shakespeare? You didn't forget *him*, did you?"

"Aw no, I laid that on 'em, too. The good-king, great-king jazz." Freddie recited his lines. Only this time, he got them all right.

"Oh, how wonderful," said Emma proudly. "You deserve applause, Freddie."

As if by magic, at that very moment the sound of clapping echoed from the rear of the empty theater. "There he is," a voice shouted through the darkness. "I knew he'd come back."

Emma and Freddie stared down the aisles as a man rushed toward the stage. "It's him," Freddie whispered. "The guy who yelled at me last night."

"The producer!" said Emma excitedly. "I told you I was right."

"Hurry up, Alonzo," the man shouted as he ran. "We've gotta catch him before he leaves again."

"I'm coming," shouted another voice from behind. It was a short, fat man with long curly hair, sideburns and tight, faded jeans. He came puffing down the center aisle.

"Who's he?" whispered Emma. "Another producer?"

"Never saw him before," Freddie mumbled. "Sure looks weird."

"Really Jerry," puffed the fat man, "all this fuss for a cat. It's indecent."

"Not just a cat," Jerry argued. "A gold mine! Just what the agency needs."

"Maybe he's signed already," said Alonzo. "If he's as great as you say . . ."

"I called Animal Talent Scouts this morning," said Jerry, jumping on stage. "They checked through their 1,500 clients. Not one is called Bitterman."

"How's he know my name?" Freddie whispered. "And who's this guy Alonzo?"

"Let's wait and see," said Emma. "Sit still and look theatrical."

Freddie sat motionless, his beach hat on his head, a toothy grin on his face, and Emma perched on his back.

"Look at that cat," said Jerry proudly. "Right out of *Alice in Wonderland*."

"I'm trying to," huffed Alonzo, climbing on stage. "Give me a hand." Jerry helped the fat man up. "Much obliged," he said, glancing at Freddie and Emma. "So this is your discovery, eh, Jer? Seems to have a bird stuck on him. Is it real?" Alonzo pinched Emma's tail. She let out a loud chirp, then fluttered to the other side of Freddie's shoulder. "I'll be darned. It *is* real. You didn't say anything about a bird, Jer. Don't work with birds. Can't keep them in focus; keep fluttering around."

"Never mind the bird," said Jerry. "It's the cat we're interested in. He'd be great to sell a dozen things. Kitty litter, fur coats. We've got another Morris here, if we play our cards right."

"Who's Morris?" whispered Freddie to Emma. "And who's this guy Alonzo?"

"He must be signed already," Alonzo repeated. "That outfit he's wearing and that tacky pigeon. It's too theatrical for an amateur."

"Here, read the article yourself," said Jerry. He pulled a newspaper from his pocket and handed it to the fat man. Alonzo read the column, then threw the paper to the ground. "Guess you're right," he said.

Emma leaned over to read the article. It was in *Variety*, the big show business newspaper. On page three, a snapshot of Freddie on stage headed up the center column. Quietly, she read it aloud:

TENNESSEE'S CAT GETS COMPETITION
PRODUCER DENIES PUBLICITY STUNT

At last night's opening of the revival of Tennessee Williams's play, *Cat on a Hot Tin Roof,* the audience got a bonus. After the curtain came down, a peculiar incident occurred. A *real* cat, dressed in a straw hat and tattered tie, jumped on stage. He pranced around, screeched and howled, then rolled over several times. One first-nighter swore he saw the animal actually perform ballet. Another said he thought he heard it sing. But before anyone could figure out what had happened, the cat mysteriously disappeared.

Questioned at Sardi's afterward, the producer, Harold King, said he knew nothing about it. "You must be crazy!" he told a reporter. Despite his denial, several people feel Mr. King deliberately created this publicity stunt to stimulate interest in his production.

One spectator, Jerry Fatima, an advertising executive with Foote, Bone & Schnelling, tried to corner the animal. Unfortunately, it escaped out a back exit. Mr. Fatima requested anyone knowing the identity of this cat to please contact him at his agency. "I've been looking for a cat like that for my commercials," he explained. "But it's hard finding one with personality. This cat had it! That back-alley look consumers love. If he's not signed already, I want to make him a star!"

Freddie's eyes grew large as he listened. "A star!" he sighed.

"I don't understand," said Emma. "They never mentioned your acting. This Jerry person isn't a producer at all. I think we should leave, Freddie."

"Oh no, Em. I'm staying. My picture's in the paper. This guy's gonna make me a star."

Alonzo circled the stage, walking around the two animals. He twizzled his hair through his fingers, then stared at Freddie. "Definite possibilities," he said, nodding. "Great face for close-ups. Let's bring him over to F.B. & S. They're casting that milk commercial this afternoon. But that hat's got to go. And that pigeon's definitely out." Alonzo grabbed the newspaper, rolled it up and swatted Emma with it. Startled, she fluttered toward the rafters, almost burning her wings on the spotlight. The fat man chased after her.

"Never mind the bird," said Jerry. "Let's take the cat and go."

"Freddie, don't go with them!" Emma chirped. "Run, Freddie, run."

"It's okay, Em," he screeched. "They're gonna make me a star!"

Jerry snatched the cat in his arms and jumped off the stage. "C'mon," he shouted. "Foote, Bone & Schnelling can't be kept waiting."

"Don't worry, Em," called Freddie as they whisked him out the door. "I'm gonna be famous."

The next moment, Emma was alone in the darkened theater. All that was left of Freddie was his beach hat lying empty in the center of the stage.

Had it been a nightmare? Emma wasn't sure. Sadly, she returned to the ledge alone, wanting only to rest and forget.

But as she sat down on her roof, every sparrow and pigeon from 99th Street suddenly began fluttering above her head. Emma stared up in surprise. Cheeping and chirping, they began dropping tiny strips of colored paper from their beaks. Their tribute of confetti sprinkled down around her, like technicolored rain.

"Surprise!" they all shouted.

"It's a party, Em," chirped Clarence proudly. "Look around."

Emma glanced at the ledge. Hung festively along the roof were bits of colored string stuck down with sticky-tape. Maude's half-filled red balloon dangled from the center. Spread on a paper napkin were bits of popcorn, danish pastry, bread crusts and muffins. A paper cup with Queen Ann's lace made the centerpiece. Tucked on the side wall was a half-torn piece of loose-leaf paper, on which Willie had scrawled, YOU DID IT!

"Congratulations," Clarence shouted.

"You did it, teech," chirped Roscoe.

"Mom made a star," Maude twittered.

"I knew you'd do it, Ma," said Willie.

"Most impressive," Monica cooed.

"Let's eat," said Sanford.

Emma sat speechless.

"Where's Freddie?" asked Clarence. "Didn't he come with you?"

"I know," said Maude. "He's taking off his makeup."

"Or signing autographs," Willie suggested.

"Was it exciting?" asked Monica. "Oh, I wish I'd been there."

"Let Emma catch her breath," said Clarence. "It's not easy making a star; I oughta know."

"How'd you like our surprise, Mom?" asked Maude. "It was my idea."

"But I made the graffiti," said Willie. "When famous people come to town, folks always throw graffiti."

"Confetti," said Emma with a leaden voice. "Confetti. Strips of paper or ribbon thrown out at festivals. Graffiti are crude inscriptions that mess up buildings and subways."

"Sure is a mess," Sanford agreed. "Such a fuss for nothing."

"What d'ya mean?" said Clarence. "My Em's not *nothing*. She made a star! I'd like to see you do that."

Hearing the pride in Clarence's voice, made Emma feel even worse. His words fell with a thud on her heavy heart.

"So where's the star?" asked Sanford. "I don't see him."

"Tell him, Em," said Clarence eagerly. "Go ahead."

Emma glanced around the ledge. The birds all perched in anticipation. "Well," she began in a cracked, trembly voice. "I was swatted. Then Freddie was catnapped. By Jerry and Alonzo."

The birds stared.

"What'd she say?" mumbled Roscoe.

"Who's Alonzo?" asked Clarence.

"I'd rather not discuss it," said Emma coolly. "Thank you all for coming."

"What about the party?" asked Roscoe.

"Yes," she said. "Well—it was lovely. Thank you."

"Okay guys," said Clarence, coming to his wife's defense. "I think Emma needs some shut-eye. Let's get together later instead."

"Some party," grumbled Sanford. "Should've stayed in bed."

"Who's gonna help clean up the graffiti," asked Willie.

"Later, kid," said Roscoe sullenly. "Right now, it looks like rain."

The Madison
Avenue Cats

During the cab ride across town, Freddie sat on the back seat. His heart was pounding with anticipation. When they arrived on Madison Avenue, Jerry scooped him up in his arms and carried him into the lobby of an immense building. Hundreds of people scurried toward dozens of elevators. Alonzo ran puffing along behind. They all squashed into an elevator and got off on the thirty-second floor. They stepped out into a deeply carpeted entry room, where giant brass letters on the wood-paneled wall announced: FOOTE, BONE AND SCHNELLING.

"Mr. Schnelling back from lunch yet, Betsy?" asked Jerry, passing the reception desk.

"Not yet," she said, glancing at Freddie. "But we've already got a roomful of cats. Wranglers have been dragging them in all morning. I counted seventeen already."

"But this one's special," said Alonzo. "He's Jerry's new discovery."

Freddie meowed and smiled at Betsy.

"Not another of your discoveries, Jer," she sighed. "When are you going to learn? That cow you cast was a real loser; almost killed the cameraman."

"This cat's different," Jerry argued. "He's a natural. He *wants* to act."

"No kidding," she said glumly. "Well, he sure looks different. Where'd you find him. In an ash can?"

"That gruff exterior's *personality*," snapped Jerry.

"Well, they're piling up in Conference Room Three. Go right in."

Jerry and Alonzo hurried down the hall and opened the doors of the conference room. Inside, seated around on leather sofas and chairs, several people sat waiting with their cats. There were Siamese, Maltese, Russian Blue and Persian; Burmese, Manx and Angora; long haired, short haired; tabby, striped and calico. It was the largest collection of cats Freddie'd ever seen. Each was poised, groomed and purring with self-confidence. Freddie felt like a slob next to such fancy, classy cats.

A marmalade cat came over to sniff him. "Who are *you*?" he asked. "I haven't seen you at a casting call before."

"My name's Freddie. Jerry just discovered me."

"Oh," he said with disgust. "An *amateur*." He walked away to curl up on the rug.

"Don't mind Felix," said the Siamese. "He's been padding through agencies since he was a kitten. Never made the big time, though. Tell me Freddie, who're you with? Professional Pets? Zany Zoos, Inc? Animal Associates?"

"I'm with Jerry. And Alonzo."

"Yeah, but what's your background, kid?"

"Oh," said Freddie. "I've been trained by Stanawhosky."

"Never heard of him."

"Isn't he the way-out guy who works with snakes?" asked the calico.

"No," said the Siamese. "That's Lester. He only handles elephants."

"Stanawhosky," Freddie repeated. "The famous actor and director. Emma says he's the master."

"Still never heard of him," said the Siamese. "What commercials has he made?"

"None."

"No commercials?" asked the Siamese in disbelief.

"Just like I said," repeated the marmalade cat. "An amateur."

"It's really disgraceful," hissed the calico. "After all my years in the business, I have to audition with an amateur."

"Cool it, Frisky," said the Siamese. "We all know you're a big deal. Frisky here's been Miss Purr Pretzel Lady three years in a row. It's gone to her head."

"Don't forget Tabby-Tiddy-Bitties," added the calico. "My face on every can. Not to mention four awards."

"You've won awards?" asked Freddie.

"Certainly," said Frisky proudly. "I've got an Addy, a Clio, a Lulu and a Spike."

"You have?" asked Freddie. "Gee, that sounds important."

"And four straight years of residuals," she added. "Plus my own social security number."

"Is that good?" he asked.

"You better believe it. But here I sit, auditioning with an *alley cat*."

"Don't put down alley cats," screeched a tabby

from the corner. "Remember Morris, honey. You're not half as big as he is."

"Who's Morris?" asked Freddie.

"You don't know Morris?" asked the marmalade cat. "My heavens, you *are* green."

"I heard Jerry mention him," said Freddie. "He said *I* could be another Morris. What does that mean?"

"Morris is the big time, kid," explained the Siamese. "Numero Uno."

"That's right," added the tabby. "He scratched his way to the top the hard way. He was a mangy drifter, roaming around Chicago's back alleys, pulling fish heads out of garbage cans. But now, he's a star. Makes $175 a day."

"Is that true?" asked Freddie in amazement.

"Sure is," said the Siamese. "Years ago, Morris was down on his luck. The Humane Society found him starving in a cellar and brought him to their shelter. An animal trainer found him there and turned him into a star. He's even been on 'The Johnny Carson Show.' "

"No kidding," said Freddie. "I watch Johnny Carson. I do my ballet while he's on."

"Your what?" asked the Siamese.

"Never mind," said Freddie. "Tell me more about Morris."

"Nothing more to tell. Morris is one in a million.

While us guys scratch around for a ten-second spot, he's got it made."

"Speak for yourself," said the calico. "Personally, I feel quality is better than quantity. My twenty-second spot for Tabby-Tiddy-Bitties was marvelous. It may win a gold medal."

"I didn't know there was so much work for *cats* in television," said Freddie.

"Why sure," said the Siamese. "Most folks won't watch commercials unless there's a furry something-or-other running around in them. They go *crazy* for us. Take this Moo-Goo-Milk commercial, for instance. It's a real nowhere product. F.B. & S. has been trying to unload it for years. They've had ads with old ladies, kids, housewives, even a cow. Can't sell a drop. But the sponsor finally wised up. They're going to use a cat. Us cats can sell *anything*."

"*Some* of us can," said the calico.

"Personality is what counts in commercials," said the Siamese. "The way things look is important; not how they really are."

"Stanawhosky says no actor should portray anything he hasn't felt inside," said Freddie.

"What does he know?" said the calico, scornfully. "Has he ever won a Clio?"

"Guess not. But Emma, my teacher, told me . . ."

"I don't know your teacher, kid," said the Siamese.

"But I do know advertising. Creativity's a waste of time unless it *sells*. Push that product, kid. That's what it's all about."

"What about serving art?" asked Freddie. "And Shakespeare?"

All the cats stared at him. "He sure is an amateur," they agreed.

Betsy, the receptionist, opened the door of Conference Room Three. She popped her head inside. "Mr. Schnelling will see you fellows now," she said.

Jerry grabbed Freddie in his arms, and he and Alonzo hurried from the room.

"Don't forget, kid," called the Siamese. "Dump that Shakespeare jazz. Just show your pearly whites and push the product."

The Contract

Irma Bitterman was terribly upset. Freddie was *gone*! She'd looked all over the house but couldn't find him. "He's run away, Herbert," she sobbed. "Or been kidnapped. Are you sure you locked the door before we left?"

"Calm down, Irma. He probably went for a stroll."

"A stroll?" she screeched. "You know how Freddie hates the streets. They scare him. Oh, Herbert, what if our baby's gotten lost; or run over, just like his poor mother? He's been acting so weird lately—dressing up and singing. Should we call the police?"

"Have you checked the ledge?" asked her husband. "Sometimes, Freddie plays with the birds out there."

"I've looked everywhere," she sobbed. "The closets, the drawers, the hamper, the fire escape. I even had the superintendent check the roof. All he found were some strips of paper and old English muffins. Something awful's happened to our Fredsy-Wedsy, I just know it."

Once again, Mrs. Bitterman checked underneath the beds and sofas. She poked into every possible place Freddie might be hiding. Nothing. Looking under the kitchen table for the third time, she spied his uneaten bowl of Pussy Pellet Balls. "That does it, Herbert," she said frantically. "I'm calling the police."

"What'd you find?"

"It's what I *didn't* find," she said solemnly. "Freddie's *beach hat*! He's worn it constantly ever since he found it. It's gone, too."

"Irma, the police are busy people. They don't have time to look for a cat's hat."

"It's not the hat I want," she shouted. "It's Freddie. Do you want our baby to wind up in some glue factory? What are police for if they can't protect our cats?"

Nervously, Mrs. Bitterman began dialing the police emergency number. Just as she reached the third digit, the doorbell rang. She dropped the phone and ran to answer it. Standing in the doorway were Jerry, Alonzo and *Freddie*. He was tucked neatly into Jerry's arms. All three were grinning broadly.

"My baby!" shouted Mrs. Bitterman, snatching Freddie from Jerry's arms. "You've found my baby. Oh, my Fredsy-Wedsy, where have you been?"

After several minutes of confusion, Mrs. Bitterman calmed down. Mr. Bitterman brought in some tea and crackers, then everyone sat down in the living room. Freddie curled up in his favorite corner of the sofa.

"We're lucky Freddie had his address tag on his collar," said Mr. Bitterman, pouring the tea. "Where'd you fellows find him?"

"At the Morosco Theater," Jerry explained. "I saw him there last night. I had a hunch he'd return today."

"*The Morosco Theater?*" gasped Mrs. Bitterman. "Where he was born? How'd Freddie find his way there?"

"You mean you don't *know* about this?" asked

Jerry. "I thought for sure you did. You two look like a couple of old vaudevillians. Ever been in show business?"

"My husband's retired from the railroad," said Mrs. Bitterman.

"I don't get it," said Alonzo munching a cracker. "If you folks didn't set up this stunt, who did?"

"What stunt?" asked Mrs. Bitterman, growing suspicious.

"Could've been a 'Candid Camera' bit," said Jerry. "Those jokesters are everywhere."

"What are you talking about?" she asked. "What's going on?"

"Let's start at the beginning," said Jerry. He pulled the copy of *Variety* from his jacket. "Read this," he said.

Mrs. Bitterman read the article. She passed it to her husband, then reread it. "That's our Freddie, all right," she said. "But how'd he get downtown?"

"He must've gone while we were out last night," said Mr. Bitterman.

"But why?" she asked, glancing at the cat. "What does it mean?"

Freddie sat curled on the sofa, his eyes closed, pretending sleep. Slowly, Jerry and Alonzo explained in detail all that had happened that afternoon.

"Mr. Schnelling was quite impressed," said Jerry.

"You should've seen Freddie in his office. He strolled right in and jumped on the old guy's desk. Then he gave him a big toothy grin, stuck his ears up and started to purr."

"That's right," added Alonzo. "Old Schnelling was really thrilled. So was the sponsor. They think Freddie's got the perfect image for Moo-Goo-Milk."

"But we've gotta act fast," Jerry cautioned. "There's lots of sharpies in this business, out to give us the knife. We should start shooting tomorrow. Since the sponsor killed the cow, we've got no time to lose."

"Knifing and shooting?" said Mrs. Bitterman. "Killing cows? What kind of funny business are you boys in?"

Freddie began to grow impatient. If only they'd let *him* explain it to the old lady. Killing the cow meant Moo-Goo-Milk wasn't going to use a cow as an advertising symbol any more. Taking shots meant they wanted photographs of Freddie as their new symbol.

After much explanation, Mrs. Bitterman finally began to understand. "I don't know," she said. "My Freddie in the show business? Somehow, it doesn't seem right. Child stars lead such unhappy lives. Margaret O'Brien was *always* crying."

"Listen, Mrs. Bitterman," said Jerry. He took two

aspirin from a pillbox and washed them down with tea. "I haven't launched a good campaign in six months. It's the ax for me pretty soon. I'll have to sell my house in Darien. Freddie's the big break I need. With him, I can make it to the top of the barrel again."

"You really think he has talent?" asked Mr. Bitterman. "He's always seemed like a plain old cat to me. A little screwy maybe, but ordinary."

"Of course he's got talent, Herbert," snapped his wife. "You've seen him dance. I've heard him sing. These boys know their business. Like they said, Freddie's one in a million."

"But Irma, I thought you didn't like the idea."

"I never said that. I just want to be sure it's right for Freddie."

"Have you really seen him dance?" asked Alonzo. "I read that in the paper, but I didn't believe it."

"Oh, he dances," said Mr. Bitterman. "Ballet, mostly. Irma says it's salami, but she's wrong. Even without salami, I see him dance."

"He uses face powder, too," said Mrs. Bitterman proudly. "And he loves to dress up. I guess it's in the blood. His mother was a theater cat, you know. That's why he's always wearing funny hats and making faces."

"But Irma, you said he was going *crazy!*"

"That's before I understood," she said. "Now it all makes sense: wearing makeup, singing, dancing. Everything my Freddie does is for a reason. He's been trying to tell us how much he wants to act."

"Then you'll agree to the deal?" asked Jerry.

"That depends," said Mrs. Bitterman. "What would Freddie have to do? You aren't going to hurt him, are you?"

"Oh, no. Performing animals are given the best of care. He just has to be himself."

"That's right," Alonzo added. "First, we'd like to start with some magazine ads for Moo-Goo-Milk. If they catch on, we'll put him in a TV commercial."

"TV?" asked Mrs. Bitterman. "My Freddie on TV? Where everyone could see him?"

"Yes ma'am," said Jerry. "Moo-Goo-Milk is a million-dollar account. They spend a fortune in TV each year."

"They'd have to," said Mr. Bitterman frowning. "I've tasted that product. It's awful. Remember, Irma? Moo-Goo-Milk is that sticky stuff in cans. Even Freddie wouldn't drink it."

"You're right," she said. "Oh dear, I'm afraid it won't work out, young men. Our Freddie doesn't like that product."

"Don't worry," laughed Jerry. "He doesn't have to *drink* it. We just want people to think he does."

"Picture this," said Alonzo. "The sun's rising over the roof of a rustic old farmhouse. There's an old red barn in the distance. We hear the sound of cows mooing. Out in the field in the morning sunlight, a farmer is plowing by the sweat of his brow. Inside the kitchen, the smiley-faced farmer's wife is setting down a hearty breakfast of bacon, eggs and Moo-Goo-Milk. She pours the delicious liquid from an earthen pitcher. Laughing, rosy-cheeked children come running downstairs, begging for their morning glasses of Moo-Goo-Milk. They drink it. They smile happily. Slowly, the camera shifts to the whitewashed front porch. There we see Freddie, happily dancing around his morning bowl of Moo-Goo-Milk. He pauses, then smiles into the camera. He lifts his head in song. There's a big close-up of his happy, grinning face. The voice-over announces: "Moo-Goo-Milk! Fresh from the farm. The healthy way to start your day.""

"Why, that's beautiful," said Mrs. Bitterman. "A whole little story, isn't it?"

"*Product identification*," explained Jerry. "That's the key. We want Moo-Goo-Milk to become an image children grow up with. Just like Betty Crocker."

"Suppose they don't like the stuff, either?" asked Mr. Bitterman.

"We'll make them," said Jerry. "At least, we'll

make them buy it. People don't know what they like anyway; you have to tell them. I've got a gut feeling for this product. I've studied graphs and market research. I know the audience pre-testing devices. I've read opinion poles and psychological studies. I've talked with P.R. men. Every product needs a hook, and Freddie's it. With him, we'll have every kid in the country crying for Moo-Goo-Milk!"

"That's not nice," said Mr. Bitterman. "Those poor crying children."

"Oh, it's fair," said Jerry. "After all, we *entertain* them. Competition in the market place: that's what made our country great."

"I see," he said. "And you think our Freddie can get people to try your product?"

"I know it!" said Jerry.

"When would he start?" asked Mrs. Bitterman.

"The sooner the better. Alonzo would like to take some trial shots tomorrow. If things go well, we can have print ads ready next month. Then we'll start work on a commercial."

"That soon?" she asked. "But there's so much to do. I'll have to give him a bath and clip his nails. He needs a new collar, too. Maybe one with rhinestones. And a hat. He's lost his hat."

"We'll take care of those details," said Jerry. "I'll stop by tomorrow morning and pick Freddie up.

Now, if you'll sign this one-year contract and model release, it's a deal."

Jerry took a form from his pocket and handed it to Mrs. Bitterman. She read it. "So much money?" she asked with surprise. "Our Freddie's going to make such money? Why Herbert, that's more than your monthly pension."

"I told you," said Jerry, smiling. "You've got a *star* on your hands."

Freddie simply purred with pleasure. He was a star at last!

A Star Rises

Everything Jerry promised came true.

As the weeks passed, Freddie was hustled from one office to another; from TV studios to photography sessions. He met with producers, copywriters, art directors, creative consultants, creative management, copy art and TV traffic representatives. He smiled for tons of vice-presidents. He posed for still shots, storyboards and promotional material. He heard about budgets and deadlines, probability samples and brand indices; the FTC and the SAMI. He learned the difference between a slow-dissolve, close-up, zoom, pull-back, stop-motion, voice-over and lip-synch. He knew about two-color, four-color and b&w ads, too. He knew how to pose for the camera, face the main light and step on his mark.

Overnight Freddie had become the new marketing symbol for Moo-Goo-Milk. Pictures of his grinning face were plastered on billboards, posed in magazines and glued across cans. The sponsor was thrilled with it all. Alonzo was given the go-ahead on his TV farmhouse commercial. After ten days of shooting, it was completed. Almost immediately, a test market was set up in Evanston, Illinois. Six times a day, Freddie's dancing feet appeared on all the local kiddy cartoon shows.

Everyone loved Freddie. Everyone fussed over him. His teeth were brushed, his fur shampooed and clipped. He ate fresh salmon every day and heavy cream whenever he liked. Jerry had a special leather box made for him. It had gold initials, F.M.B., across the front. Mrs. Bitterman bought him a real fur coat with booties, to protect his famous dancing feet.

And Freddie loved it all. But it was hard work. The toughest part was grinning all the time. Freddie could

grin standing up, sitting down, on his back, on his
haunches, even in his sleep. Sometimes, after a long
day's work, his mouth was so stiff, he couldn't close
it. Every night, Mrs. Bitterman tippy-toed into the
kitchen where Freddie lay on his fur blanket in his
wicker bed. "Look Herbert," she'd say smiling down
at him. "See how Freddie's grinning? He must *love*
being a star!"

And so he did. Already, he was a big celebrity on
the block. Each morning when the limousine drove
up to take him to the studio, neighbors would gather
on the corner. "There goes Freddie," they'd call.
"The big TV star."

Freddie would stick his wet nose against the window of his handsome leather case. He'd grin and
show his shiny teeth. Freddie grinned all the time
now. After all, that was his job.

After three months, the campaign was finally complete. All pictures had been taken; all cans had been
covered. TV spots were placed and magazine ads
printed. At last, Freddie could have a well-deserved
vacation.

On Freddie's first morning home, Miss Ivers rang
the bell. She was carrying a warm plateful of corn
muffins. "They're for our star," she whispered. "Give
him some before he goes to work."

"He's asleep right now, Edith," said Mrs. Bitterman. "Besides, Freddie can't eat corn muffins any more. They take the shine off his teeth."

"Oh, that's sad," said Miss Ivers. Curiously, she glanced around the room. "I didn't see the limousine this morning. Is something wrong?"

"Oh no," explained Mrs. Bitterman. "Freddie's milk campaign is finished at last. He's home for a while."

"How wonderful, Irma. When will we see him on TV?"

"Not for a few weeks, Edith. His commercial is only being shown in Illinois now. They have to test market it there first."

"You don't say," said Miss Ivers, nibbling a muffin. "How's that done?"

"Different ways," said Mrs. Bitterman. "It's such a science. Those advertising boys explained it. Women like green cans and men like blue. And everyone loves lemon. If a product's got lemon in it, *everybody* buys it."

"But Freddie's selling milk, not lemons."

"And women buy round packages more than square ones," Mrs. Bitterman continued. "But they like pictures on them. Photographs. That's why they're using Freddie. He takes such a sweet picture. Oh, those researchers even have housewives save their trash. They pick it over, you see. To find what people buy. But they're testing my Freddie's commercial with sweat."

"With what?"

"Sweat," Mrs. Bitterman repeated. "It's really cute, Edith. They get lots of women in a theater and stick things on their wrists. That tests their rate of perspiration. When they sweat a lot, that means they like it."

"You don't say," said Miss Ivers, opening the door. "You learn something every day."

"Don't forget your muffins, Edith," called Mrs. Bitterman.

"You eat them," she answered. "I've just lost my appetite."

As Miss Ivers closed the front door, Freddie suddenly awoke from his sleep. He rolled over in his wicker basket and slowly opened his eyes. He yawned, glancing down at his well-clipped claws. A speck of soot stuck to his middle nail. He flicked it off. Freddie took a dainty nibble of his salmon, lapped his cream, then wiped his chin on the kitchen towel. He stretched himself and strolled through the hall. Glancing into the mirror, he grinned. His pearly white teeth smiled back at him. His rhinestone collar sparkled. His shiny fur glistened. Wow, what a gorgeous cat!

"Now then," he thought, "what should I do today?

Perhaps a visit to Miss Lucy? Won't the old gal be green with envy when she sees me? Na, she can wait. I'll take a sunbath on the fire escape."

Freddie went into the kitchen and jumped on the windowsill. "Yuck, it's sooty out there," he thought. "Can't get my million-dollar paws scrunged up. Guess I'll visit the old birds instead. Haven't seen the gang in months."

But Freddie suddenly reconsidered. "What would we talk about?" he wondered. Now that he was famous, he'd nothing in common with pigeons any more. Besides, it was dirty on their ledge. And cold, too. "Ah well," he thought, "can't afford to get the sniffles and ruin my career. A nice day at home is the best idea."

Freddie returned to the hall. He looked into the mirror again. He grinned. Wow, he was gorgeous. In all the world, there was no finer cat than F.T.C. Superstar!

Old Acquaintance

It was a bright January morning when the first snow of the season fell on Riverside Drive. Great tufts of it hung from the heads of the stone lions on the 99th Street cornice.

Emma Pigeon woke up and blinked her eyes. The morning sun glistened on the white landscape of New Jersey. What a glorious day. How thrilled the children would be to see the snow. At last they could play their hide-and-seek game in the playground. (One team set out, carefully leaving a trail of claw tracks for the other to follow.)

But what would Emma do today? Go to the library? No, she'd been there four times this week. Already, she'd learned about tie-dying and the Russian Revolution. My, she missed the magazines Freddie used to bring her. Especially *National Geographic*.

More than that, of course, she missed Freddie. Emma hadn't seen him since he'd been catnapped. She's waited all night for his return. But he had never come.

Naturally, Emma knew of Freddie's sudden stardom. Often, she'd seen the limousine parked outside. Then Freddie, in his fancy leather case, would be escorted into it.

"You made him what he is today," Clarence always argued. "And now he snubs you like you don't exist."

"He's so busy," Emma would insist. "But he'll come by soon."

"I oughta go down and nip him in the nose," Clarence would threaten.

"I'm sure he'll visit us soon," Emma would insist.

But Freddie never came. Three months had passed. Still, he hadn't come.

"Hey Em, it's snowing!" shouted Clarence, waking up and shaking his feathers.

"Yippee!" chirped Willie. "Let's get the gang for hide-and-seek."

"Come with us, Mom," coaxed Maude. "You're great at finding tricky places."

"I'd rather not, dear. Perhaps tomorrow."

"Wanna join me and Roscoe at the skating rink?" asked Clarence. "There'll be enough chestnuts for three."

"Not today." She sighed. "I think I'll read a while instead."

"Suit yourself," said Clarence. "I'll bring back some nuts for dinner."

"That's fine, dear," said Emma, waving a wing good-bye. She watched as Clarence flew east and the children fluttered to the playground. Emma stared at the water several minutes. Snowflakes fell, then quickly disappeared. She sighed, once again thinking of her friendship with Freddie. That, too, had disappeared.

Shaking her feathers, she quickly flew up to her office to read. But there was nothing new or interesting in her files. My, how she missed those magazines. Emma glanced toward the corner and saw the glasses Freddie had given her. How they brought back memories. Was it only a few weeks ago that she and Freddie had sat here under the stars, rehearsing through the night? It seemed more like years.

Hopping along her plastic weatherproofing, Emma

stared down at her theater file. Through the falling snowflakes she saw the page that lay on top. It was Freddie's favorite line from Shakespeare. Emma read the words: "Good king, great king,—and yet, not greatly good." A single tear dropped from her lid and mingled with the snowflakes. "Ah well," she sighed, shaking her feathers. "It's *still* a lovely day."

A week went by and Freddie's vacation continued. He drank his cream, ate his salmon and kept his claws free of soot. Each day, he sat by the hall mirror for hours. He checked his teeth to be sure they sparkled. He practiced all his grins. He kept his tail well fluffed.

The Moo-Goo-Milk Company had sent Freddie six complimentary cases of their product. Freddie's grinning face was on every can.

Each morning, Mrs. Bitterman checked the mail to see if any news had come from the advertising agency. Nothing yet. She began getting anxious. "I hope we hear something soon, Herbert," she said. "I think Freddie's getting nervous, too."

"He's getting fat," said Mr. Bitterman. "And snooty."

"I think he needs some fresh air," she said. "Come here, Fredsy-Wedsy, love."

Mrs. Bitterman snapped on Freddie's fur coat, and slipped on his fur booties. She opened the kitchen window. Then she stretched his white fur blanket on the snow-covered fire escape and placed him in the center.

Freddie rested there for almost an hour, enjoying his sunbath. About two o'clock, Emma Pigeon happened to fly by. But she didn't notice Freddie. All that white fur above the snow made Freddie invisible.

As Emma fluttered by, she peeked into Freddie's kitchen window, hoping to catch a glimpse of her old friend. She hadn't seen his limousine for days and wondered what was wrong. As she hopped along the lumpy tufts of snow, one of them began to move. Emma was startled. Suddenly, Freddie turned his head and saw her resting on his white fur hood. "Hi Em," he said. "Whatcha doing up there?"

Emma flushed with embarrassment. "Why Freddie, I didn't see you."

"It's my new fur coat," he said. "How d'ya like it? Pretty jazzy, huh?"

"Why yes," said Emma. "Quite elegant."

"Yeah, only the best for me. I'm a star now."

"So I've heard," she said coolly.

"Oh sure," he bragged. "It's all over the neighborhood."

"I'm really happy for you, Freddie. Our hard work finally brought you success."

"That's not what did it," he said. "I don't do that silly Stanawhosky stuff no more. It don't go on Madison Avenue."

"No Stanislavski?" asked Emma in surprise. "What *do* you do?"

"This," he said proudly. Freddie sat up and grinned broadly. He wiggled his nose and showed his sparkly teeth. To Emma, it looked like a silly empty-headed smirk. "That's all you do?" she asked. "Just smile?"

"Not *just* a smile," snapped Freddie. "It's the million-dollar Moo-Goo-Milk grin. It's gonna make kids cry all across the country. Like Betty Crocker. I'm Jerry's hook!"

"I don't understand," said Emma. "I thought you were acting."

"Acting doesn't count," said Freddie. "Just personality. I've got it. Not everyone can sell a product, you know. Folks don't like to look at fat ladies or guys with moustaches. They want cats instead."

"They do?"

"Why sure," said Freddie. "Ya see, Em, you had everything all mixed-up. Theater's not the place for cats. Commercials is where it's at. I'll be another Morris soon. Numero Uno. Wow, I'm glad I met Jerry. Without him, I'd be nowhere."

"Oh really," snapped Emma. "I hadn't realized I had wasted so much of your time."

"That's okay," said Freddie. "You didn't know any better. I got my big break anyway. Right now, ladies all over the country are sweating just for me."

"They are?"

"Why sure. Moo-Goo-Milk was nowhere until I showed up. I'll probably get a Clio or a Spike. Wow, I wasted my time with hard work. Now, I just grin and make a fortune. But I'm worth it. Jerry says I'm one in a million."

Emma blinked. "Yes," she said curtly, "well, I have to go now."

"Oh sure," Freddie yawned. "I've gotta get my beauty sleep. See ya around."

"I don't know what's happened to him, Clarence," Emma chattered that night. "Freddie says he's Morris Crocker. He wants to make children cry. He's got hooks and spikes, and he's waiting to hear from sweaty ladies."

"He's a Frankenstein!" said Clarence. "Just like that guy in the Classic Comic. You made yourself a monster, Em."

"No dear," Emma corrected. "Frankenstein was made from bits and pieces of dead flesh."

"More than he deserves," snapped Clarence. "I oughta go down and nip him in the tail."

"And he never uses Stanislavski," Emma added.

"Stanawhosky?" asked Clarence.

"That's just what Freddie said," murmured Emma. "Oh dear, I don't understand any of it."

Birds of a Feather

As the days passed, Freddie and the old folks patiently waited for news from the agency. Each morning, more complimentary cases of Moo-Goo-Milk arrived. The Bitterman's kitchen floor was filled with them. Every closet was stacked with them. But still, no word about Freddie's commercial.

After another week, Jerry finally called with some

news. "Things are looking great," he told Mrs. Bitterman. "Our test market results from Evanston, Illinois just came in. Freddie's comercial has only been on three weeks. Already, Moo-Goo-Milk sales have risen 28 percent!"

The Bittermans were thrilled. Well, Mrs. Bitterman was.

"I don't like it," said Mr. Bitterman. "Freddie's not the same cat any more."

"Of course he isn't," said his wife. "He's a star now. I must bring him down to Irma and share the good news. Put on his booties, Herbert. I'll look for his rhinestone collar."

"It's not natural," Mr. Bitterman grumbled as he snapped on Freddie's fur coat. Freddie grinned and showed his pearly whites.

When they arrived downstairs, Miss Ivers was thrilled. "Why Freddie dear," she smiled. "I'll take you right in to see Miss Lucy. She'll be so pleased."

"Hi, old girl," said Freddie, strolling into Miss Lucy's room.

"Why, Frederick," she purred. "Enchanting to see you. But I'm afraid I look a sight. I've had a dreadful cold. My eyes are still puffy from those nasty bacilli."

"Ya do look kinda swollen," he agreed.

"But you look *marvelous*." She smiled. "Absolutely distinguished."

"Ain't it the truth." He grinned. "Sorry I couldn't make it down before this, Loo, but I've had a rough schedule."

"I understand," she said. "It must be frightfully tiring being a celebrity."

"That's a fact," said Freddie. "Most folks think it's all bright lights and glitter. But they're wrong. Those lights sure make you sweat."

"Oh, you must be careful," she cautioned. "Sweat —uh—perspiration leads to chills."

"Yeah, I've gotta watch it. Can't let the sponsor down by getting sniffles. I'm their hook."

"How delightful," said Miss Lucy. "I hear you have a leather carrying case with your initials in gold."

"Fourteen karat," he said proudly. "Come up and see it sometime."

"And what do you plan to do with all that *lovely* money?"

"Well, I got me this fur coat. Booties, too."

"Quite proper," said Miss Lucy. "A cat of your position must dress appropriately. Only the best."

Freddie nodded. It sure was swell talking with Miss Lucy. She understood a classy guy like him. He should've come visiting sooner. Freddie cuddled up on the rug beside the Persian. He sniffed. There was an unpleasant, medicinal smell in the room. "What's that?" he asked, screwing up his nose.

"It's my vaporizer," said Miss Lucy, pointing to the dresser. "I'd be lost without it. Keeps my nasals open, liquifies my eyeballs. You should have one, too."

"Yeah," he said. "My eyes need to be shiny for commercials. Just like my teeth. Have ya seen my teeth, Loo?" he asked, grinning broadly.

"Such jewels," purred Miss Lucy. "No wonder you're a star. I'd no idea you had such prize-winning molars."

"My old lady brushes them every day," he bragged. "Twice on Sunday."

"And so she should. A cat is nowhere without proper grooming."

"Right," said Freddie. "But it's hard keeping clean with so much soot around."

"*Ecch*," said Miss Lucy. "Don't mention the word. It's disgusting. This whole city's one big filth ball."

"Now that I'm a star, I'm gonna move the old folks outa this dirty place. Maybe I'll get an air-conditioned penthouse with a doorman."

"Oh, but I'd hate to see you leave, Frederick," she purred. "You're the only animal with poise in the entire building. Not at all like those ruffian alley cats and scruffy birds."

"They're not all bad," said Freddie. "Emma Pigeon

is a nice old gal."

"How loyal of you," said the Persian. "Sticking up for a tacky old bird. But they're all the same, my dear. Positively *ruin* the look of a building. Those feathers flying. So unsanitary."

"Emma's ledge *is* messy," Freddie agreed. "She collects all sorts of junk up there; books, papers, cups, scraps, pine cones . . ."

"Not pine cones!" screeched Miss Lucy. "Frederick, your allergy! Keep away from that dreadful bird or you'll look like a bowling ball."

"Aw, we don't see each other any more," he said. "I'm too busy to bother with birds."

"I certainly hope so," she insisted. "A pigeon friendship could destroy your image. Oh Frederick, I'm so eager to see you on TV. Miss Ivers will wheel the set into my room when you come on. But tell me about this marvelous product you're selling."

"It's called Moo-Goo-Milk. Comes in cans."

"Well, it's done wonders for you," she purred. "Your fur's so silky now."

"*I* don't drink it," said Freddie. "I don't like it. I just sell it."

"Oh? Is that quite proper, Frederick?"

"Listen, Loo, facts don't count. Just figures. I show my pearly whites and push the product. That's how I got to the top."

"I see," she purred. "How clever of you. No wonder you're successful."

"You bet," Freddie agreed. "Jerry says if I can sell Moo-Goo-Milk, I can sell anything. And he's right. Remember how I sold you into eating those . . ."

"You did what, my dear?" she asked.

"Aw, never mind," said Freddie. "It's not important."

"That's right," she agreed. "What's important is that you're a star."

"Not just a star," he corrected. "F.T.C. Superstar."

"Exactly, my dear," she purred, breathing into her vaporizer. "Now that you're a celebrity, you really must try my brand of bath oil. It does wonders for the follicles."

"Don't mind if I do, Loo" said Freddie, inhaling the mentholated vapors. "Gotta watch my follicles."

Late that night, Freddie felt really rotten. Had he eaten too much salmon? Sniffed too many vapors? As he lay in his wicker basket underneath the kitchen table, he rolled his eyes in restless sleep.

Piled against the kitchen walls were crates of Moo-Goo-Milk. Stacked along the countertops were cans of Moo-Goo-Milk. Across each can, box and crate was plastered a picture of Freddie's grinning face. Hundreds of Freddie-eyes stared back at him. Thousands of Freddie-teeth grinned down at him.

Then suddenly, the boxes started to *move*! They crawled from the closets. They rolled from the tables. They bounced off the counters. They leered their sappy grins. They showed their pearly whites. Then, swaying back and forth, the giant chorus of Freddie-cat-cans began to chant: "PUSHTHEPRODUCT! PUSHTHEPRODUCT! WHATALIAR! WHATALIAR! PUSH-THEPRODUCT! PUSHTHEPRODUCT! WHATALIAR! WHAT-ALIAR!"

The army of Moo-Goo-Milkers began to march. Clinking and clanking, they drew closer. And closer! Rows of wobbly stacks climbed into Freddie's wicker basket. Within minutes, Freddie was completely crushed beneath a ton of grinny-tin.

Freddie shook himself and woke up in a cold sweat. His stomach ached and his head throbbed. Wow, what a nightmare. He'd never had an awful dream like that before. Really crazy.

As Freddie thought about the dream, he realized many parts of it were true. He *was* a liar. He'd lied to Miss Lucy about his allergy. He'd lied to Emma about his great day-boo. And now, he was lying to *everyone* about Moo-Goo-Milk. Well, so what? He *had* to lie. That was part of being a star. F.T.C. Superstar!

Final Sale

Freddie spent the next two days inside his wicker basket—brooding. He didn't eat. He didn't sleep. He didn't even clean his nails. He was too upset. On the third day, he dragged his basket out into the hall. He couldn't stand looking at those Moo-Goo-Milk cans any longer. They all kept *staring* at him.

Mrs. Bitterman was upset. "He's acting strange again, Herbert. Just like in September."

"How can you tell?" sighed her husband. "Anyway, I've got something to cheer him up. Fan mail. The postman brought it this morning."

"Herbert, you're not going to read Freddie's personal mail?"

"Why sure," he said, tearing open the letters. "Don't expect him to read it, do you?"

Freddie weakly looked up from his basket as Mr. Bitterman began reading aloud:

DEAR FREDDIE CAT,
I see you a lot on TV. You come after the cartoons. My mom says I shouldn't watch cartoons. She says I shouldn't watch you, either. She don't like commercials. They get you to buy stuff you don't need. But I like you. You have a cute fussy tail. I'm gonna make my Mom buy your milk. Did you know your picture is on the can?"

YOU'RE REAL CUTE,
Cynthia Weinstein

DEAR FREDDIE BITTERMAN,
You're the nicest cat on my TV. I love your smiley face. I never saw a cat dance. How is it done? With strings? My grandma bought some Moo-Goo-Milk because you told us. She put it in her coffee. But she didn't drink it. I had some in my pudding. But I didn't like it. I'm glad you like it. You look real happy when you drink it. I don't think we'll buy it any more. But I still like you very much.

YOURS TRULY,
Ricky Sanchez

HEY FREDDIE,

How much do they pay you to sell that goo? No amount of dough could make me drink it. I just wrote a new jingle for your commercial:

Moo-Goo-Milk
Will make you sick,
Dump it in the garbage
Quick, Quick, Quick!

My father is in consumer research. I told him all about your product. He's checking it out.

BETTER WATCH IT,
Marni Norstrum

TO FREDDIE THE CAT,

Stop drinking that gunko junk! You're a nice cat, but that milk is awful. Dad says everything on TV is gunko junk. Is that true? You must love Moo-Goo-Milk a whole lot. I see you drink it all day long. I hope you don't get sick. *I* did!

GOOD LUCK,
Jonathon Parker

"Please don't read any more, Herbert," said Mrs. Bitterman. "What awful letters. None of those children like our Freddie's product."

"That's because it stinks, Irma."

"But Mr. Fatima said their sales rose 28 percent."

"Sure they did," he said. "People *love* Freddie. But that milk still stinks."

"Yes," agreed his wife. "I bet Freddie could sell ice

to Eskimos. But those boys and girls seem to think the milk is *poison*."

Mr. Bitterman glanced at the hundreds of cans stacked in the kitchen. "So it's not poison. It's not *good*, either."

"What'll we do, Herbert. Our Freddie loves the show business. And all that money."

"But he doesn't need it, Irma. Already, he's got a fur blanket, coat and booties. And a diamond collar."

"Only rhinestone."

"Whatever."

"Oh, I wish Freddie could tell us what he wants." She sighed. "I don't like our cat selling junk."

"*Gunko* junk," her husband added.

"But I hate to end his career," she said. "He loves it so."

"Well," said Mr. Bitterman. "If any cat could talk, it would certainly be our Freddie."

The old folks nodded. They glanced over at Freddie seated in his wicker basket. They stared at him and waited. Freddie glanced back at the old folks. This was his big chance. They expected to hear from him. Freddie stared into their eyes. Then he looked at the tons of Moo-Goo-Milk cans piled high in the kitchen. He remembered his nightmare.

Quickly, he bounced from his basket and jumped onto the kitchen table. With his paws, he began knocking the cans to the ground. One by one, they rolled along the kitchen floor, until there was just one left. Freddie picked up the last can, rolled on his back, then ripped the label from it with his teeth. He chewed it up and spit it out into the trash can.

"Did you see that, Herbert?" said Mrs. Bitterman. "Freddie's trying to tell us something."

"That's a message, all right," agreed her husband. "Freddie doesn't want to sell that junk anymore."

"*Gunko* junk, Herbert."

"Whatever."

"That settles it," she said. "I'm calling Mr. Fatima right away."

Freddie sat on the kitchen floor and began to purr. He hadn't felt this good in weeks.

"Terrific dinner, Em," said Clarence, dipping his beak into the water cup.

"Just leftovers," said Emma. "I saw a fine recipe in the trash this morning. But the magazine was too heavy to carry."

"Yeah," said Willie. "Dinners used to be more fun when Freddie brought us *Gourmet* magazine."

"Never mind," said Clarence. "Your mother's leftovers are the greatest."

"It was a breadcrumb filling," Emma said. "I would've liked to try it."

"That reminds me," said Maude. "Has anyone seen Snooty-Boots lately?"

"Snooty-Boots?" asked Emma, nibbling the last of her Cheez Doodle. "Who's that, dear?"

"That's Freddie, Ma," said Willie. "That's what the birds call him since he turned snob."

"I call him Frankenstein," said Clarence. "And I say good riddance."

"You're all too hard on Freddie," said Emma. "It's not easy being a star."

"Maybe so," said Clarence, "but I wouldn't give a nickel to see that cat. Remember how he used to prance around here all night?"

"Aw, he was cute," said Maude. "I liked that song he always sang, about the alphabet. How'd it go?"

As Maude tried to remember the lyrics, a familiar sound came drifting through the evening air. It was Freddie's voice, they were certain. And it was coming closer. The Pigeons quickly glanced toward the corner wall.

Freddie was padding his way along the ledge. He was wearing Mr. Bitterman's straw hat and he was singing:

A B C D E F G H . . . . .
I got a gal
In Kalamazoo
Don't want to boast

But I know she's the toast
Of Kalamazoo.
Going to Michigan
To see the sweetest gal
In Kalamazoo—zoo—zoo.

"Why Freddie," cooed Emma. "How nice to see you."

Freddie danced his way toward Emma, graciously gliding on his paddies. He tipped his straw hat and bowed. "Hello my dear lady," he said sweetly, taking her wing in his paw. "What a good lady. What a great lady. What a greatly good, dear lady."

"What'd I tell ya, Em," said Clarence. "He's come apart altogether. A regular Frankenstein."

"Freddie, I don't understand," said Emma blushing. "Does this mean . . ."

"That's right." Freddie grinned. "I'm my loveable self again. I've just retired from show biz."

"But Freddie," she stammered. "Your fame. Your money. Your fur booties."

"Gone, Em. The whole bundle. I left all my furs outside Miss Lucy's door along with a can of Moo-Goo-Milk."

"Tell me, Freddie, why this sudden change?"

"I finally saw the light," he explained. "I was becoming a real . . ."

"Snooty-Boots," said Willie.

"Right," said Freddie. "And besides, I wasn't having fun no more. Selling stuff is fine for some cats, but not for me. I'm too sensitive."

"I could've told you that," said Emma. "All great actors have sensitive souls."

"I couldn't sleep anymore, either," he added. "Not even catnaps."

"Yeah, sleep's important," Clarence agreed. "*I* could've told you that."

"I'm sorry for the way I acted," said Freddie. "I betcha thought I was a real. . . ."

"Frankenstein," said Clarence.

"But I'm back to normal now," he said. "Things are gonna be just like in the good old days."

"How wonderful," sighed Emma.

"Oh boy," mumbled Clarence.

A Star Falls

The next morning, Mr. Fatima came to visit. Freddie was resting on the sofa and overheard the whole argument.

"You can't do this," said Jerry, gobbling an aspirin. "I need that cat. He's my meal ticket. Moo-Goo-Milk's a bust without him."

"We've made up our minds," said Mrs. Bitterman.

"I won't have my Freddie selling gunko junk."

"That's un-American!" Jerry shouted. "Where would this country be if we didn't sell junk? Naked and starving!"

"Maybe so," said Mr. Bitterman. "But we won't have our cat making children sick. Freddie loves children."

"All right," said Jerry nervously. "Moo-Goo-Milk stinks; I admit it. But we can still use Freddie other ways. In fact, I've got a new project all worked out. Congressman Katz is running for Governor this year. We're handling his campaign. He needs a socko symbol, and Freddie's perfect. I've already written the slogan:

> *Grown-ups love Katz*
> *Children love Katz*
> *Even cats love Katz*

We'll paste Freddie's face on a million buttons. It's a natural."

"Leon Katz for Governor?" asked Mr. Bitterman. "That crook? He's mixed-up in dozens of scandals. And he's never in the country."

"That's the one," said Jerry. "He'll need lots of help to get elected. And Freddie can give it to him."

"You mean you sell people, too?" asked Mrs. Bitterman. "Just like milk?"

"Why sure," said Jerry. "Politicians are packaged, too; just like toothpaste. It's all the same on Madison Avenue."

"That's awful," said Mrs. Bitterman. "Leon Katz is a crook. Stupid, too. I'd never vote for him. Not even if Freddie asked me."

"You folks don't understand," Jerry shouted. "Freddie's *mine*! For eight more months. We've got a legal contract, and you'll have to stick to it."

Mr. and Mrs. Bitterman stared at Freddie. Freddie stared back. They all stared at Jerry.

"What'll we do, Irma," said Mr. Bitterman.

"We can't break the law," said Mrs. Bitterman.

"You're darn right," said Jerry. "I've got big plans for that cat. Have him at the studio by nine o'clock tomorrow morning. Grinning. We'll start photographing campaign buttons right away."

Freddie's fur bristled. He was tired of being pushed around. He wasn't going to grin for dum-dum Katz. Not for a million buttons or a million dollars. Not any more!

Suddenly inspired, he jumped from the sofa and dashed into the kitchen. Freddie began meowing pitifully and rolling around the floor. He twitched his nose. He wiggled his ears. He scratched his stomach. He wailed and moaned. He scraped his back against the wall.

The Bittermans stared in astonishment. Freddie had never acted that peculiar before!

"What's that cat doing?" asked Jerry nervously.

"I don't know," said Mr. Bitterman. "It looks like he's having an attack."

"Oh my gosh," said Jerry, running into the kitchen. He stumbled over the crates of Moo-Goo-Milk stacked by the doorway. "You haven't been feeding him *this* junk, have you?" he asked. "Some cats have allergies, you know."

"No," said Mr. Bitterman. "He hates the stuff."

Freddie continued to moan and wail. He popped his eyes and stared at the old lady pleadingly. He twitched faster and scratched harder.

"Wait a minute," said Mrs. Bitterman, finally catching on. "You're right. It *is* an allergy."

"Oh no," shouted Jerry. "What a rotten time to have a fit. How long do they last?"

"For days," she said. "Sometimes for weeks."

"That's right," Mr. Bitterman added, smiling at his wife. "Sometimes for months."

"Well, what happens to him?" asked Jerry nervously. "Can he still work?"

"Oh no," said Mrs. Bitterman. "His eyes puff up and his tongue hangs out."

"Just like a piece of wet liver," nodded Mr. Bitterman.

"And his paws swell up the size of bowling balls," added his wife.

"It's a disgusting sight," said Mr. Bitterman. "We can't stand to look at him, so we put a bag on his head."

"Oh no!" groaned Jerry. "What a lousy campaign symbol. An itchy cat with a bag on his head."

"Maybe Leon Katz could put a bag on his head, too," suggested Mrs. Bitterman. "He might get more votes that way."

"What am I doing in this business?" Jerry moaned. "My mother wanted me to be a fireman! Well," he said, grabbing his briefcase, "back to the old drawing board." He glanced at Freddie who was still itching and twitching in the corner. "What rotten luck," he muttered. "That cat could've been another Morris. Even bigger." Jerry slammed the door behind him.

The old folks smiled at each other. "A nice young man," said Mr. Bitterman. "But much too nervous."

"He should've listened to his mother," said Mrs. Bitterman. "Then we wouldn't have had to fool him."

"It was for a good cause, Irma. Besides, I think Freddie *is* allergic. To Madison Avenue."

Freddie hopped on the sofa and began to purr. His old folks sure were smart!

Welcome Home

Two weeks later, Freddie got his last fan letter. It said:

DEAR FREDDIE,
I can't see you on my TV any more. I'm glad you don't sell that funny milk no more. But I miss your smiley face. My friends all liked you, too. You could have been some big star.

TAKE CARE OF YOURSELF,
Ricky Sanchez

Freddie kept the letter in his wicker basket, underneath his pillow. *Real* fan mail this time. It sure felt great.

The lovely winter weather continued. Each day, Freddie would take his sunbath as the children returned from school. "Hi, Freddie," they'd call. "Freddie was almost on TV," they'd say. "He was almost a *star*."

Freddie smiled and looked out over the white landscape of Riverside Drive. The children's sleds made lovely patterns across the snow. Just like a Grandma Moses painting. He and Emma had found a book called *Great American Painters* on the old folks' shelf. Each afternoon, they'd learn about a new artist. Freddie liked Grandma Moses best. What a great old lady.

But no greater than his own old folks. Even though Freddie wasn't a star any more, they still treated him like a celebrity. He got broiled salmon every Sunday and cream twice a week. Mrs. Bitterman turned his leather case on its side and placed it on the fire escape, for Freddie and his "friends," the birds. On cold snowy days, he and Emma hopped inside and read their books.

"Aren't they sweet, Herbert," she said as she watched. "I think they're *reading*."

"After what's happened," said her husband, "I believe *anything*. Freddie talks, too," he added. "At night when we're in bed."

"What does he say, Herbert?"

"Who knows? But it sounds like *poetry*."

And so it was. Emma had found a lovely book of poetry, which she and Freddie had memorized. He loved to recite to himself before going to sleep. "Once upon a midnight dreary, while I pondered weak and weary. . . ." Great stuff! And of course he still danced; each night, during "The Johnny Carson Show."

There were so many things to do, Freddie rarely missed show business. He'd even found a way to get rid of all those crates of Moo-Goo-Milk. There was actually someone who *liked* it. Miss Lucy! She drank the can Freddie had given her and found it delicious. Miss Ivers was so pleased, she promised to provide a lifetime supply of corn muffins in return for the Bitterman's lifetime supply of milk.

And wow, did Miss Lucy love Freddie's fur coat and booties. The perfect outfit for long winter nights curled up beside her vaporizer. She was truly grateful. In return for the lavish gifts, she allowed Freddie and Emma to borrow copies of Miss Iver's *Animal Medical Journal*. "Isn't that great, Em," said Freddie, laughing. "Now, if your kids get beak boils or feather fungus, you can cure it right away."

And though it was hard, Freddie finally confessed to Miss Lucy about his lies. Surprisingly, she didn't mind. She *liked* the Pussy Pellets, she *loved* the milk and *adored* the furs. "It's a pity you have no true allergies." She sighed. "Makes a cat more interesting. And what a shame you're no longer a star. Yet you're amazingly respectable; considering you're so common."

And so Freddie had settled back into his regular life, gladly giving up thoughts of stardom. But Emma hadn't.

"I think I've found it," she said excitedly one afternoon. She and Freddie were seated in their leather case, reading through *Variety*. "They're staging a new revival of *The Owl and the Pussycat*. It's perfect for you, Freddie. We'll type you up a new résumé. Let's list your commercial credits, too. Now, later tonight, we'll sneak up to Mr. Olson's penthouse and. . . ."

Freddie closed his eyes dreamily. He thought of his fan letter, tucked warmly inside his basket. He blinked. He stared out at the snow-covered landscape. The warm afternoon sunlight sparkled brightly. The children glided along the hillside on their sleds, making patterns in the snow. How pretty it all was. Just like a Grandma Moses painting. He yawned.

Freddie looked at his dear old friend and smiled. "Forget it, Em," he said. "I've had my moment of glory. That ain't bad for an alley cat!"